J. T. EDSON'S FLOATING OUTFIT

The toughest bunch of Rebels that ever lost a war, they fought for the South, and then for Texas, as the legendary Floating Outfit of "Ole Devil" Hardin's O.D. Connected ranch.

MARC COUNTER was the best-dressed man in the West: always dressed fit-to-kill. BELLE BOYD was as deadly as she was beautiful, with a "Manhattan" model Colt tucked under her long skirts. THE YSABEL KID was Comanche fast and Texas tough. And the most famous of them all was DUSTY FOG, the ex-cavalryman known as the Rio Hondo Gun Wizard.

J. T. Edson has captured all the excitement and adventure of the raw frontier in this magnificent Western series. Turn the page for a complete list of Berkley Floating Outfit titles.

J. T. EDSON'S
FLOATING OUTFIT
WESTERN ADVENTURES
FROM BERKLEY

THE YSABEL KID
SET TEXAS BACK ON HER FEET
THE HIDE AND TALLOW MEN
TROUBLED RANGE
SIDEWINDER
MCGRAW'S INHERITANCE
THE BAD BUNCH
TO ARMS, TO ARMS, IN DIXIE!
HELL IN THE PALO DURO
GO BACK TO HELL
THE SOUTH WILL RISE AGAIN
.44 CALIBER MAN
A HORSE CALLED MOGOLLON
GOODNIGHT'S DREAM
FROM HIDE AND HORN
THE HOODED RIDERS
QUIET TOWN
TRAIL BOSS
WAGONS TO BACKSIGHT
RANGELAND HERCULES
THE HALF BREED
THE WILDCATS
THE FAST GUN
CUCHILO
A TOWN CALLED YELLOWDOG

J.T. Edson

.44 CALIBER MAN

BERKLEY BOOKS, NEW YORK

This Berkley book contains the complete
text of the edition.
It has been completely reset in a type face
designed for easy reading, and was printed
from new film.

.44 CALIBER MAN

A Berkley Book / published by arrangement with
Transworld Publishers, Ltd.

PRINTING HISTORY
Corgi edition published 1969
Berkley edition / April 1980

For information address: Transworld Publishers, Ltd.,
Century House, 61–63 Uxbridge Road, London W5 5SA.

ISBN: 0-425-04620-6

A BERKLEY BOOK® TM 757,375
Berkley Books are published by Berkley Publishing Corporation,
200 Madison Avenue, New York, New York 10016.
PRINTED IN THE UNITED STATES OF AMERICA

For John Wayne,
a .44 Magnum Caliber Man

Chapter One

The eerie flat slapping sound of a bullet passing close over his head caused Lou Temple involuntarily to duck it down. Faintly, over the drumming of his four-horse team's hooves, the creaking and jingling of the stagecoach's harness, almost drowned by the rumble of the wheels, he heard the crack of a rifle-shot. Experience gathered fighting Yankees during the War Between The States helped him to locate the man who had fired in his direction.

Even while looking, Temple prepared to urge the team on at a faster pace. The bullet had come over the rolling country on the right of the trail and ahead of the stagecoach, from a distance of at least two hundred yards. It might easily be the prelude to an attempted hold-up. If so, Temple hoped to run by the robbers at top speed before they came closer to the trail.

Sitting alongside the driver, the guard hefted his ten-gauge shotgun and also scanned the country to the right in search of the man who had fired the shot. Being young, ambitious and new to the work, Abel Simcock hoped there would be a try at holding up the stagecoach in the course of which he might distinguish himself.

Neither of the men found difficulty in discovering their assailant. However, the sight caused Simcock some concern. Deadly as a double-barrelled ten-gauge shotgun might be at close quarters, it was sadly inadequate over a distance of two hundred yards.

Especially when matched against a rifle. However, if the man who had shot planned to hold up the stagecoach he had a mighty strange way of going about it. He stood on a rim in plain sight, waving the rifle in his right hand over his head. Hanging by its horn in his left hand was a double-girthed saddle with a bedroll fastened to its cantle. Dressed in all black clothing, from low-crowned, wide-brimmed Stetson through bandana, shirt, levis pants, to his boots, he had a gunbelt of the same colour about his waist. In addition to the rifle, he carried a revolver butt forward in the holster on the right of his belt and a sheathed, white-handled knife hung at the left. Not an unusual armament in Texas during the late 1860s. He was not masked in any way, but the distance prevented the guard from making out his features.

Much to Simcock's surprise, Temple started to slow down the team instead of encouraging it to go faster. The guard had heard of drivers working in cahoots with hold-up men, but Temple did not strike him as being of that treacherous kind. On the rim, the black-dressed figure swung the saddle on to his left shoulder and started walking towards the trail.

'That's a Henry he's toting, Lou,' Simcock warned, hefting the shotgun to a more convenient position. 'It could be a stickup.'

If the driver felt concern over the approaching man carrying a repeating rifle, he failed to show it. Hauling back on the reins, he stopped the horse and raised his right foot to shove home the brake-handle.

'Could be winter, only it's not yet gone spring,' he told his guard laconically as the coach came to a halt. 'Put up the scatter, you won't need it.'

'He took a shot at us,' Simcock reminded, making no attempt to obey.

'The hell he did,' scoffed Temple. 'If he'd been shooting at us, either you or me'd have lead in us by now. For Tophet's sake do like I say and put up the scatter. That feller'd send a bullet down each barrel and one a-piece up your nostrils happen you try to point it his way.'

'You know him?'

'I wouldn't be telling you to put the scatter down if I didn't. Wonder how come he's out thisways and afoot?'

'Who is he?' demanded Simcock, still keeping the cocked shotgun ready for use.

'The Ysabel Kid!'

For a moment the guard stared into Temple's leathery sardonic face. Then Simcock turned his gaze towards the approaching figure. Already he had come close enough for Simcock to distinguish various details. The revolver was a walnut-handled old Dragoon Colt and the knife's dimensions hinted that it might be of the kind Arkansas blacksmith, James Black made for Colonel Jim Bowie. According to all accounts, the man named by Temple carried such weapons.

From the gunbelt, Simcock raised his eyes to the head under the Stetson. He saw an Indian-dark face with an almost babyishly innocent cast of features. Or so he thought until he met the other's scrutiny. The red-hazel eyes which studied Simcock were anything but babyish or innocent. They bore a glint of reckless devilment, having seen life—and bloody, sudden death.

A stranger to Texas might have wondered how so innocent a face came to have such eyes. Simcock did not need to ask, despite his youth and inexperience as a stagecoach guard. During the past few years he had heard much about that tall, slim, harmless-appearing youngster called the Ysabel Kid. Enough for him to set the shot-gun's hammers into the half-cock position and return it hurriedly to its boot. While he no longer feared a hold-up, Simcock felt that Temple had only slightly over-called the dangers of pointing his weapon in the newcomer's direction.

Born in the village of the *Pehnane* Comanche, the Kid's father had been a wild Irish-Kentuckian and his mother the daughter of a Long Walker, war leader of the Dog Soldier Lodge. His mother had died giving birth to him and, his father being away much of the time on horse-hunting and later smuggling missions, he was raised as a Comanche.* Long Walker had taught him to read tracks, to be adept at concealment and locating hidden enemies, how to capture and control horses and all the other things a *Pehnane* warrior needed to know. Before he reached his fifteenth birthday, he had the rifle-shooting skill of a Kentucky hillman and knife-fighting ability which came from his maternal Comanche–Creole blood. Not fast with his Dragoon Colt, by Texas standards, he could still perform adequately when using it.

The War Between The States prevented the Kid from having to choose between his white blood and loyalty to the Comanche. At first he and his father rode with Mosby's Raiders, their Indian-trained abilities as scouts being much appreciated by the Grey Ghost. However, the Ysabels' talents became more urgently needed in their home State. So they returned to spend the last year of the War transporting urgently-needed supplies—run through the Yankee Navy's blockading squadron into the Mexican port of Matamoros—north across the Rio Grande. It had been tough, dangerous work, for there were many people eager to lay hands on the valuable shipments put in the Ysabel family's care.

During that time and after the end of the War, when the work they did once more became smuggling, the Kid had built up a reputation as a deadly-dangerous fighting *man*. However, word had it that, since his father's death, the Kid had retired from smuggling and gone to work on Ole Devil Hardin's great OD Connected ranch.

Not that the Kid's smuggling connections caused Simcock any concern for the safety of the stagecoach or its passengers. As soon as the guard learned the black-dressed youngster's identity, he stopped worrying about the rifle shot being part of a plan to halt and rob the coach. Except among the men hired to suppress it, smuggling as carried out by the

*Told in *Comanche.*

Ysabels had never been regarded as a crime. Along with most folks in Texas, Simcock thought of it as a protest against an unfair infringement of personal liberty imposed by the Yankee Government.

'Howdy,' the Kid greeted, coming to a halt at the side of the trail. He looked even younger as a cheery grin creased his face. 'Got room for another one, Lou? My hoss stepped in a prairie-dog hole back there a piece and I didn't cotton any to the notion of walking down to Fort Sawyer.'

'Swing up your saddle, Kid,' Temple offered. 'There's room for you ins—— Hey! You mean you've lost your old Nigger hoss?'

Sympathy showed on the driver's and guard's faces, for the Kid's big white stallion had become almost as legendary as its master. However, the Kid showed none of the distress they might have expected to see at such a loss. Instead he seemed both amused and annoyed at the suggestion.

'Ole Nigger's too slick to go stepping into prairie-dog holes,' he stated. 'It was one of my mounts from the ranch.'

A Texan used the word 'mount' for the horses allocated to him when working on a ranch. It seemed, from what he had just said, that the rumours concerning the Kid's new employment were true. However, Simcock was given no time to comment on the matter. Climbing on to the roof of the coach, he reached down ready to accept and secure the Kid's saddle.

Having given all the explanation he, the driver or guard considered necessary, the Kid approached the coach. He became aware that the passengers were watching him through the windows. Two were female, a pretty girl wearing a sun-bonnet and cheap coat over a gingham dress and an older, beautiful, well-dressed woman. Behind them the Kid could see a handsome young man with brown hair and a trim moustache, but made out little of how the other was clothed. In fact the Kid paid little attention to his future travelling companions. Resting his rifle against the right front wheel of the coach, he prepared to pass his saddle up to the waiting guard.

Gripping the cantle in his right hand and still retaining his grip on the horn with his left, the Kid swung the heavy rig towards Simcock. Once the guard took hold of it, he realised that there must be considerable strength in the lean, wiry young frame. Taken with the bedroll, the coiled Manila lariat, headstall, bit and reins fastened to the horn, the saddle weighed over fifty pounds. Yet the Kid had carried it a fair distance and still handled it with comparative ease. Once he had handed his property to the guard, the Kid retrieved his rifle.

'Howdy, folks,' the Kid greeted, opening the coach's door ready to enter. 'Sure hope I didn't spook you none, shooting over Lou's head thatways.'

'You come mighty close to spooking me,' the driver assured him.

'Wasn't any other way I could let you know I needed a ride, Lou,' the Kid explained. 'I'd only just then topped that ridge and reckoned you might not see me or hear me shout.'

'A man could get shot doing what you done, Kid,' Simcock chided, securing the saddle to the roof.

'I wouldn't have chanced it, only I saw you nursing a ten gauge,' grinned the dark-faced youngster. 'Allowed I was out of scatter-gun range and took a chance.'

With that the Kid started to swing into the body of the coach. He glanced with renewed interest at the women. They sat facing each other on either side of the door he passed through, yet it hardly seemed likely that they were travelling as companions. Small, petite, the girl had a sweet, innocent face that showed a healthy, out-of-doors tan. From her clothes, she was a rancher's daughter and not a rich one. Somehow she seemed vaguely familiar, but gave no hint of recognising the Kid. She had a preoccupied, worried expression as she sat back in her seat.

If the girl enjoyed an open-air life, the woman

most certainly did not. Although her clothing showed signs of travel and hard use, they had originally cost good money and were cut to a daring, figure-hugging style no 'good' woman would wear. From the dainty, impractical hat perched on her blonde head and the make-up on her face, the Kid figured her to be a saloonworker, or a theatrical performer, travelling between jobs.

Finding the girl and the blonde sharing the stagecoach came as no surprise to the Kid. Such vehicles offered the fastest form of public transport across the Texas range country and were available to anybody with sufficient money to purchase a ticket. So 'good' and 'bad' women sometimes found themselves travelling together on the same stagecoach.

Not that the Kid devoted his attention to the women. His eyes went to the man and he came to a halt just inside the door, staring with amazement. Experienced in many aspects of life though the Kid might be, he had never seen anything like the way the male passenger was dressed.

At least six foot in height, the man exuded a rugged charm which went well with his wide shoulders and powerful frame. He did not appear to be wearing a gun but that fact alone, strange as it might be in Texas, failed to account for the normally unemotional Kid's reaction at seeing him.

The man wore a jacket and vest of some rough-looking homespun material, yet well-tailored to set off his physique, a white shirt and black string tie, ordinary enough to warrant no notice. It was from the waist that his clothing differed radically. Below a broad leather belt with a large silver buckle, he wore what appeared to be a woman's skirt. Coloured with black, blue and green squares slashed by red and yellow lines, the 'skirt' left the man's knees bare. Thick stockings of the same check pattern covered his powerful calves, ending in stout, untanned boots. What looked like a folded blanket of the same colourful material as his 'skirt' slanted around his torso from the left shoulder, partially concealing the fancy hilt of a long-bladed knife sheathed at his right side. Suspended about the man's waist and hanging in front of his 'skirt' was a pouch larger, but something like those used to carry bullets for muzzle-loading rifles. It was fancier than a bullet-pouch, being made from the skin of a black and white animal and secured with a large silver catch. On the seat beyond the man was a round brimless black hat with a silver badge of some kind, from under which an eagle's feather slanted rearwards, fixed to its side.

So interested in the sight was the Kid that he hardly noticed the hilt of a small knife which showed from the top of the stocking on the outside of the man's right leg.

'I wouldn't say anything, cowboy,' the blonde warned, following the direction of the Kid's gaze. 'Scottie there doesn't take kindly to folks hoorawing his clothes.'

Although the woman began to speak with an amiable condescension, she lost it when the Kid turned his face towards her. Going by first impressions, she had taken him for the usual run of range-country youngster. The feeling left her as the Kid's red-hazel eyes met her gaze. Young he might be, even if a touch older than she had first imagined, yet he was anything but the gauche country hick she originally thought him. April Hosman knew men, they were her business, and figured she had better avoid selling that Indian-dark youngster short. Doing so could be dangerous.

'Obliged for the warning, ma'am,' the Kid replied.

The coach lurched into motion before he could say more, causing him to sway and sit down hurriedly alongside the girl. Looking to see if he had struck her with the rifle in jolting down, he found he had not and felt almost certain that he recognised her. In turn she glanced at him, a half-smile playing on her lips. Her face bore lines of grief and the eyes were tired. After a moment the smile died away, to be replaced by a slight, resentful frown.

'Damn that Lou Temple,' the Kid began, then he

noticed a reddish-brown curl of hair showing from beneath the sun-bonnet. 'Well I'll swan! You're Trader Schell's gal, Jeanie.'

'Yes,' she agreed, sounding a little bitter.

'Damned if I knowed you, all fancied up this ways,' the Kid grinned. 'How's Ma and your pappy'n Kenny? I ain't run across them in a coon's age.'

Somehow the Kid formed the impression that the words were not wholly welcome. He wondered if the girl had taken offence at his reason for failing to recognise her. Maybe she did not care to be reminded that on their previous meetings she had been dressed in boy's clothes. From what he remembered of Jeanie Schell, he doubted if that alone was the answer. She had always been a merry tomboy, with an impish sense of humour and an explosive, soon-come-soon-gone temper. Instead of cussing him out for his forgetfulness, her lips quivered a little and her eyes blinked like they tried to hold back tears.

'Ma and Kenny're fine,' she replied, then sucked in a deep breath and continued. 'Likely you haven't heard—— Pappy was killed a couple of months back.'

'I hadn't heard,' the Kid admitted contritely. 'I'm real sorry I asked about him like I did.'

'It was a hoss,' Jeanie said quietly, blinking her eyes again. 'The best-looking and meanest critter we'd brought in since that big paint stallion Pappy sold to Ole Devil Hardin.'

Silently cursing himself for starting the conversation, the Kid wondered how he might end it without adding to the girl's grief.

'It'd have to be a real mean hoss to lick him, Jeanie-gal,' he said gently. 'Your pappy was a forty-four caliber man.'

'Thanks, Kid,' Jeanie answered, a hint of pleasure and gratitude creeping into her voice and onto her face. Then the bitter lines returned. 'There're some who don——'

The words died away and Jeanie turned to look out

of the window. Moving into a more comfortable position on the seat, the Kid wondered what had brought out the girl's lost, unfinished sentence. Trader Schell had been a mustanger, catching and breaking wild horses, well-liked by the people who bought stock from him, even though a shrewd businessman. However, Jeanie showed no inclination to resume the conversation and the Kid did not consider himself a sufficiently close friend to force the matter further.

Hefting the rifle in his hands, the Kid looked for some way to avoid nursing it during the journey to Fort Sawyer. The Overland Stage Company had foreseen the need and fitted hooks to the woodwork above the seats on which travellers could hang their shoulder arms. Before the Kid could rise and make use of the hooks, the young man sitting opposite him indicated the rifle and asked:

'Would that be a Henry you have?'

'Sure,' the Kid agreed, trying to recall where he had heard such an accent as the man used.

'I've never seen one with a wooden foregrip before,' the man commented. 'All the Henrys I've seen have a bare metal barrel and magazine.'

'This here's one of the new model,' the Kid explained with an air of conscious pride. He held out the rifle so that the man could see the slot let into the right side of the brass frame. 'You load it through here in the breech instead of pulling the tube open.'

'That's an improvement,' the man said soberly. 'The magazine was always the Henry's weak point. This new model looks a stouter gun all round. I haven't seen any of them on sale yet.'

'Or me,' the Kid admitted. 'I got this 'n' for helping a salesman who was taking a whole slew of the old model Henrys to Juarez.'*

Although it later gained fame as the Winchester Model of 1866—first in a long line of successful lever-action repeaters—the type of rifle in the Kid's

*Told in *The Ysabel Kid.*

hands made its appearance on the market under the name of the New Improved Henry.

After the Kid had hung the rifle on the hooks, he talked with the man for a time about the relative merits of various firearms and discussed hunting opportunities. Although the man did not introduce himself, or say what brought him to Texas, the Kid asked no questions. However, the Kid felt that he had been sufficiently sociable to satisfy his curiosity on one point.

'No offence, friend,' he said. 'But do all the folks dress this fancy back where you come from?'

'It's a kilt, cowboy,' April Hosman put in, following the direction of the Kid's gaze. 'Folks in Scotland wear them.'

'The gals too?' asked the Kid, for he had never seen a saloongirl dressed in such a short garment.

'No!' the man replied shortly, his voice losing its friendly note. 'The kilt's not worn by women.'

Remembering how the young Scot had dealt with a loafer who made opprobrious remarks about his appearance in Brownsville, April felt that she had better intervene. Sure the Scot had proved capable of defending himself with his fists but she doubted if the Texan would fight with his bare hands.

'I've heard that you can tell which family a man belongs to by the colour of his kilt,' she remarked. 'Is that right?'

'It's true enough, ma'am,' the Scot agreed and tapped the kilt with his left forefinger. 'This is the tartan of the Clan Farquharson. My name is Colin Farquharson, of Inverey.'

'You're a tolerable long ways from home, friend,' the Kid commented, trying to remember where he had heard the name.

'Aye,' Colin agreed. 'A kinsman of mine came home singing the praises of Texas, so I thou——'

The crack of a rifle-shot, mingled with the scream of a horse in pain, chopped off the young Scot's words. Lurching violently, the coach came to an abrupt halt. The body pitched and rocked against the thorough braces, the tough straps of heavy leather which connected and supported it above the draught and running gear.

Taken by surprise, the Kid and Jeanie were thrown off their seats and across the coach. The Kid landed on top of Colin and Jeanie collided with April. Outside another shot sounded and one of the men on the roof gave a croaking cry. Before the Kid could untangle himself from Colin, the left side door of the coach jerked open.

Chapter Two

After halting to pick up the Kid, Temple kept his team moving at a steady trot along the Fort Sawyer trail. With over six miles separating them from their destination, neither the driver nor Simcock discounting the possibility of danger. The guard stayed alert, although he left his shotgun in the boot, studying each clump of mesquite, bushes, hollows in the grounds, draws and ridges for signs of lurking enemies.

For all that, the attack when it came took them both by surprise. At that point the trail ran straight, with fairly open land on either side. Despite this careful scrutiny of places behind or among which a man might hide, Simcock saw nothing to disturb him. All in all the terrain did not lend itself to laying an ambush. There were rocks and other places that could conceal waiting men; but none sufficiently large to hide their horses. There was a draw maybe half a mile from the trail where mounted men might wait. If it should hold a gang, Simcock figured they would be no great danger. Between his shotgun and the Ysabel Kid's rifle, the owlhoots would pay dearly for trying to rush the stagecoach.

Simcock was still thinking on those lines when a rifle cracked from among a clump of mesquite about a hundred yards to the right of the trail. So well hidden that the guard failed to detect him, the man shot accurately. Raked through the neck by the bullet, the off-side lead horse went down screaming.

Instantly everything was in a state of confusion. Dragged off balance as its mate went down, the near leader almost fell. The off wheeler reared on its hind legs, trying to avoid running on to the stricken animal ahead. Even as the coach swayed violently, Temple's training sparked off an automatic reaction. Booting home the brake, he hauled back on the reins in an attempt to regain control of the team.

Only by catching hold of the hand-rail and bracing his feet against the sloping front of the driver's box as the coach slammed to a halt did Simcock avoid being thrown from his seat. During the violent lurch of the body, Simcock caught a movement from the corner of his left eye. He turned his head to look closer as the thorough braces returned the body to its normal position. At first he thought that his eyes were playing tricks on him, for what he took to be a rock not far from the left side of the trail began to move.

Agitating briefly, the rear part of the 'rock' began to rise. It proved to be a blanket covered with dust until the same colour as the real rock. Swiftly the man under the blanket stood up and flung it aside. Dressed in the style of a *vaquero*, he was bare-headed and his face showed more Indian than Mexican blood. Gripping a fancy-looking Navy Colt in his right hand, the man sprang towards the coach.

At the same moment, on the right of the trail, a tall, slim Mexican lurched into sight. He had been crouching behind a small rock, covered with cuttings from the nearby bushes. Not far from him a tumbleweed began to move, although there was hardly any wind and it had previously been motionless. Thrusting it aside, a third man appeared from a hollow in the ground over which it had been lying. Shorter and more stocky than the Mexican, he was of the same race. They wore fancy, expensive charro clothes and were alike in the expressions of evil and lust on their faces. Leading four horses, a rider came from the distant draw and headed for the clump of mesquite which sheltered the man with the rifle.

Aware that he had achieved his ambition and become involved in a hold-up, Simcock thrust himself erect. Cursing himself for not drawing the shotgun earlier, he wasted no time in trying to do so. Instead he sent his right hand fanning to the butt of the Army Colt holstered on his belt. Even as he made his play, he remembered that a rifle had killed the horse. Neither of the men on the right could have used it, for they had been hidden within twenty yards of the trail.

Before Simcock could draw his Colt, the rifle spat again from among the mesquite. Lead ripped into the guard's body. Giving a cry of pain, he twisted around and tumbled over the left side of the box. Fully occupied with controlling the team, Temple could do nothing to try to fight off the men. Springing in from the left, the half-breed jerked open the door at his side. While the taller man lined a Starr Navy revolver at Temple, his companion approached the body of the coach.

Looking into the barrel of the half-breed's revolver, the Kid eased himself from Colin. Then the right side door jerked open and the smaller Mexican's Navy Colt ended any chance of immediate resistance. Jeanie wriggled off April's lap and darted a glance at the Winchester then to the Kid. Giving an almost imperceptible head shake, the dark youngster awaited developments.

'Don't kill them unless you have to, Indio,' the stocky Mexican ordered, in Spanish. 'Somebody'll maybe pay to get some of them back.'

'*Si*, Jaime,' the half breed answered. 'If they make a wrong move I'll only kill them a little bit.'

'Is the guard dead, Indio?' called the taller man, without turning his Starr away from Temple's direction.

'Looks like it, Adán,' replied the half breed, glancing down and back into the coach too quickly for the

Kid to take advantage of it. 'He's not moving and bleeding bad.'

'Get them out so I can look at them, Jaime,' ordered Adán.

'Com' out here, peoples,' Jaime said, using English for the first time. 'You don' make trouble and we don' hurt you,'

Which was, as the Kid for one of the passengers well knew, a lie. The only reason they had not been shot immediately was that the *bandidos* wanted to see if any of them would be worth holding for ransom. Once that had been established, the worthless male passengers and driver would be killed. Hardened to the worst aspects of life though he might be, the Kid did not care to think about the fate of the two women before death finally claimed them.

Yet he knew that resistance at that moment would be suicidal. Even outside there would be small enough chance, but being in the open offered more opportunity than did the confines of the coach.

Trained from birth to think fast, analyse situations and rapidly work out solutions, the Kid put his lessons to good use. There was one way he might get a break. Slender, risky as hell, but a whole heap better than no chance at all.

'Do what he says, ma'am,' the Kid said, looking at April.

'Have we any choice?' the blonde answered, rising and picking up her vanity bag from where it had lain between her and Colin. 'Don't let us women-folk stop you making a move. We both know what they'll do to us—and it's no pleasure that way.'

Backing off, still covering the door of the coach with his Colt, Jaime watched the blonde come to it. If April felt any concern, she managed to hide it. Showing surprising agility, she swung herself down from the coach.

'*A la derecha!*' Jaime ordered, and April moved to her right, halting by the rear wheel.

'I'll go next,' the Kid decided. 'Then you, friend. You'll be the last one out, Jeanie-gal.'

'Sure, Kid,' the girl answered, before Colin could speak. 'Pappy had a Henry and I've used it.'

'That'n works the same way,' the Kid told her and went to the door. 'Don't do nothing rash, gal.'

While dropping to the ground, the Kid glanced around and felt relieved at what he saw. During his border smuggling days he had gained an almost encyclopedical knowledge of Mexican *bandido* gangs. Probably he had never heard the words *modus operandi*, but he knew what they implied. The killing of the lead horse from a distance, followed by the appearance of men hidden close to the object of the robbery, had always been the way in which the Flores brothers' gang worked.

One glance at the taller Mexican confirmed the Kid's guess. He was Adán Flores. The other brothers, Tiburcio, Matteo and Vicente, did not appear to be on hand. In fact only five of the gang showed themselves; three by the coach and the horse-holder waiting for the rifleman to mount up over by the distant clump of mesquite. Five, not twenty or more; and commanded by Adán, by far the least efficient of the family. Given just a smidgin of good Texas luck, something might be done about busting up the robbery.

Recognition was mutual. Taking his eyes from Temple, Flores looked the Kid's way, grinned and said, '*Hola, Cabrito*. We not know you were on the coach.'

'You should have asked before you stopped it,' the Kid replied, speading Spanish with the accent of a border-country Mexican and moving to stand at April's side.

Flores let out a bellow of laughter. 'You hear that, Jaime? We should have asked before we stopped it. *Cabr*—— *Madre de dios*, what's this?'

The sight of Colin framed in the doorway brought the words popping from Flores' lips. Remembering his own feelings when confronted unexpectedly by the kilted Scot, the Kid had been counting on Colin's appearance to distract the *bandidos*. The hope only partly materialised. While Flores and Jaime ogled with bugged-out eyes, the latter still kept his Colt pointed straight at the Kid's belly. There was also Indio in the coach and the two approaching riders to be considered. So the Kid stood still.

On the driver's box, Temple had managed to quieten down his team. Seeing Flores was no longer watching him, the driver started to edge cautiously along the seat towards Simcock's shotgun.

After the Kid jumped from the coach, Indio started to enter. However, the half breed gave Jeanie no chance to grab the rifle. His eyes raked her from head to toe and his thick lips separated in a slobbering lecherous grin. Dull-witted and bestial, Indio thought only of the fun he would have with the women passengers and did not look in Colin's direction. Shooting out his left hand, he caught Jeanie by the arm.

'Hey, little one,' he said. 'You real pretty. I think I take you if Adán don't want you.'

Desperately Jeanie forced herself not to struggle. The half breed would kill her at the slightest show of resistance. While death would be preferable to being carried off alive, Jeanie aimed to hold on until there was no hope of escape. Unless she missed her guess, the Kid had something in mind. So she must do nothing to spark off trouble before he was ready to make his play. The fingers left her arm, rising to stroke her face. Although she shuddered, Jeanie made no attempt to move away. Outside the coach, voices rose and she heard laughter.

'What is it, a man or a woman?' Flores whooped as Colin dropped to the ground. 'I've never seen anything like it.'

'Or me,' Jaime went on, 'Hey, *Cabrito*, what does he wear under that skirt?'

'Why don't you look and find out?' the Kid asked.

'You watch them,' Flores told Jaime. 'I'll do it. You, gringo, come here.'

'He means you, friend,' the Kid said to Colin. 'Watch how you go, he's bad mean and a killer.'

Although Colin guessed that the *bandidos* had commented on his appearance, he had not understood their words. However, he knew better than to argue in the face of the guns and so walked towards Flores. Having followed the conversation, April began to pull open the neck of her vanity bag.

'He looks real fancy, Jaime,' Flores declared as Colin came to a halt before him. 'I bet you he wears drawers like a saloongirl.'

With that Flores stepped closer to Colin. Drawing the hammer of his Starr back to full cock, he placed its muzzle against Colin's ribs. Then the *bandido* bent forward at the waist and took hold of the kilt's hem with his left hand. Grinning a little, Jaime turned his head to satisfy his curiosity. Catching April's eye, the Kid nodded slightly. She slipped her right hand into the bag. For his part, the Kid stood in a relaxed-seeming slouch but his right hand turned palm out close to the butt of the Dragoon Colt.

Hot indignation ripped through Colin as he realised what the Mexican planned to do. With a growl of fury, he brought his left hand from his side. He struck the bottom of the Starr, meaning to push it away from him, forcing it inwards and up. The result was all, and more, than the Kid had hoped for.

Adân Flores had never been a quick thinker, so the Scot's reaction took him by surprise. Feeling the Starr struck, he reacted far too slowly. By the time his brain flashed its message to the right forefinger, the gun's barrel was no longer pointing in Colin's direction. Carried up by the Scot's hand, the Starr's muzzle aimed towards the side of its owner's head.

Just an instant too late Flores realised the danger. His finger tightened on the trigger. The Starr had a double-action mechanism, but could be cocked manually. When this was done, a slight pressure on the trigger freed the hammer. So it proved. At Flores' tug, the hammer drove downwards and struck the waiting percussion cap. Flame spurted from the barrel, singeing the *bandido's* hair as the bullet ploughed into Flores' temple. Shock and disbelief momentarily twisted at Flores' face as he jerked erect. Then he reeled sideways and sprawled to the ground.

After which all hell tore loose by the halted stagecoach.

Jaime started to turn his revolver in Colin's direction, then realised the danger of such a move. One could not give *Cabrito*, the Ysabel Kid, that much of a chance and live to boast about it. So he swung his attention back to the black-clad young Texan. Only just in time, for the Kid's right hand had already gripped the Dragoon and started to pull it from the holster.

At Colin's first hint of movement, the Kid folded his fingers around the walnut butt and hooked his thumb over the hammer spur. He began to lift the gun, drawing back the hammer so as to complete the cocking by the time the barrel cleared leather. Unfortunately Jaime's attention did not stay on Colin and Flores for long enough to let the Kid complete his draw.

Seeing the Kid's predicament, April brought her hand from the bag. In it she held a Remington Double Derringer, .41 in caliber and deadly at close quarters. Going by the way she cocked and aimed the little hide-out gun, April had taken the trouble to gain proficiency in its use. The Derringer's upper barrel cracked and a hole appeared in Jaime's forehead. Dropping his Colt, he staggered around in a circle and then collapsed. There was no time for the Kid to express his gratitude at being saved.

At the sound of the first shot, Indio thrust Jeanie on to the seat and swung to face the right side door. As the half breed started to lunge forward, the girl drew up her legs and drove her feet as hard as she could into his back. Much of Jeanie's life had been spent riding horses, an exercise noted for developing sturdy leg muscles, so the kick packed some force when it landed. Caught unexpectedly, Indio pitched through the door faster than he intended. In going, he fired his gun involuntarily. Although the bullet flew harmlessly across the range, the sound of the shot alerted the Kid to the fresh danger.

Spinning around, the Kid completed his draw. Cocked already, the big Colt slanted upwards from waist level as Indio made his precipitous departure from the coach. The Kid did not hesitate in his actions; under the circumstances he dare not. With a deep bellow, caused by forty grains of powder igniting in the cylinder's uppermost chamber, the Dragoon coughed a .44 caliber, round soft lead ball along its seven-and-a-half inch barrel. Struck in the head while still in mid-air, Indio's body jerked under the impact. Although he landed on his feet, his legs buckled under him and he crashed forward, spraying blood and brains on to the ground.

Some thirty yards away, the two riders saw the trouble begin and brought the horses to a halt. Whipping up his Spencer rifle, the man who had shot Simcock tried to lay his sights on the Kid. At the same time, the other *bandido* dropped the reins of the three horses he led and grabbed at his holstered revolver.

With the attention taken from him, Temple let the team's ribbons fall and lunged across the seat. Grabbing hold of the shotgun's butt, he began to slide it from the boot and came to his feet. Continuing to turn, he caught and raised the foregrip with his left hand. Snuggling the butt against his shoulder, he looked along the twin tubes at the horsemen.

Deciding that the man with the Spencer posed the greatest threat, Temple gave him priority. The Kid still faced the coach, dealing with Indio, and April's Derringer could not be relied upon against an enemy thirty yards away. So Temple sighted on the *bandido* and sent nine .32 buckshot balls hissing his way. Through the puff of burned-powder smoke Temple saw the Spencer's barrel jerk upwards. He heard a horse scream in pain and altered his aim to the second Mexican. Startled by the bellow of the shotgun above them, the three team horses moved restlessly. The coach rocked under Temple's feet, causing him to tilt the shotgun and his second barrel's charge flew harmlessly into the air.

Spreading out after leaving the shotgun, the first cloud of balls reached their target with inches separating them from each other. Two of the balls caught the Mexican in the body, a third drove into the ribs of his mount, while a fourth raked a bloody furrow across the rump of another horse. Letting out a scream of pain, the wounded horse reared on its hind legs. With his rifle pointing into the sky and slipping from numb hands, the man slid backwards over his horse's rump. As he landed, the other injured animal kicked out. Its iron-shod hoof grazed the top of the man's head, then it went bucking and leaping across the range.

Satisfied that he need devote no further attention to Indio, the Kid swivelled around. He cocked the Colt on the recoil as he started to turn and made ready to deal with the last of the gang. Although he had shot the half-breed from waist level, aiming by instinctive alignment, he knew such tactics would no longer work. That kind of shooting was only practicable at close range. The Kid would need to use the Colt's sights. So he brought up his left hand, gripping the right as added support for the Dragoon's four-pound-one-ounce weight.

Raising the gun shoulder high and at arms' length, the Kid saw the result of Temple's intervention. That left only one of the gang to be dealt with. Even if he did not make a fight, he would ride as fast as he could to tell the Flores boys what had happened to Adán. The Kid knew what would happen then. So he took the best aim he could manage at the man, no easy matter with the horse made restless by its companions, and fired. Through the swirl of powder smoke, the Kid saw the man's horse leap violently and its rider topple sideways from the saddle.

After thrusting Indio from the coach, Jeanie bounced to her feet. Her intention of grabbing the

Kid's Winchester ended as she looked from the coach. Born and raised in frontier Texas, Jeanie could evaluate a dangerous situation and draw sensible conclusions. From all appearances, the Kid would not need his rifle. There was something else calling for more urgent attention. Jeanie felt herself the one most suitable, with the Kid fully occupied, to deal with the matter.

There might only be a few *bandidos* present, but they were sure to belong to a larger gang. So the coach had best be got moving *pronto*, headed for Fort Sawyer, before the rest of the gang arrived. However, one of the team horses had been killed and getting a replacement might spell the difference between safety and death. Maybe the *bandidos'* mounts were trained for the saddle, but one of them could be put into harness in an emergency.

Seeing the results of Temple's shotgun blast, Jeanie knew she must act fast. Not for the first time since starting her trip to Brownsville, she found herself cursing the unfamiliar garments her mother insisted that she wear. Grimly hitching up her skirt, showing her high-button boots and bare legs to above knee level, she leapt from the coach. On landing, she saw the Kid tumble the second Mexican to the ground. Without sparing a moment to announce her intentions, Jeanie sprinted by the Kid. So far the horses had not scattered and she hoped to catch at least one of them before they took off running.

Although he lay without moving, the gang's horse-holder had suffered no worse injury than a graze across his ribs. Before reaching him, the Kid's bullet had punched a hole in his mount's ear and caused it to rear. That and the pain of the close-passing bullet had tumbled the man from his saddle.

Realising that he was not seriously hurt, the *bandido* gave thought to escape. Even as he tensed to make a sudden leap for the nearest horse, he saw Jeanie running towards him. At first he could hardly believe his luck, then guessed what she planned to do. Swiftly he revised his plans. Instead of taking the risky way of trying to jump on to a horse, he would let the girl come up and grab her. With her as a hostage, the *gringos* would not risk shooting and have to let him go.

In falling from his horse, the revolver had dropped from the *bandido's* holster. He could feel it beneath his body and cautiously moved his hand until his fingers crept around its butt. Then he watched the girl coming nearer and prepared to hurl himself at her the moment she was close enough.

Chapter Three

Shock numbed Colin Farquharson as he watched Adán Flores falling away from him. For a moment he stood rigid, staring in fascinated horror at the blood which oozed from the hole in the *bandido's* temple. Then the thunder of shots brought his attention to what was going on around him. Turning, he watched the short fight rage its course. So swiftly did everything happen that Colin hardly found time to collect his startled wits. Seeing Jeanie spring from the coach and dart by the Kid jolted Colin from his daze. To him it seemed that the girl was flying in hysterical panic and running blindly into danger.

The sight spurred Colin into movement. Forgetting his revulsion at having caused the death of another human being, he raced forward at an angle which would bring him to the running girl. Even hindered by her hitched-up skirt, Jeanie raised a fair turn of speed. In fact she ran so fast that Colin only managed to catch up with her as she drew near to the horses. Noting the nervousness exhibited by the animals, Colin decided he must stop the girl before she ran among them and was seriously hurt. Flinging himself through the air, he wrapped his arms about Jeanie's waist. A startled screech broke from the girl as she felt herself caught, lifted from her feet and borne to the ground. Feeling her struggles, Colin gently but firmly pressed his torso on to her and held her down.

Guessing what Jeanie had in mind, the Kid lowered

his Dragoon. A quick look around told him everything was in hand by the coach. Although a touch pale, April still held the Derringer and seemed capable of using it again should the need arise. Up on the box, Temple was once more calming his team. So the Kid set off after the girl. He saw Colin converging with Jeanie. Before the Kid could say or do anything, the Scot had tackled her. A grin twisted the Kid's lips as he thought of what Jeanie would say when Colin released her. Then he saw something which drove all the levity from him.

From his position on the ground, the *bandido* had been unable to see Colin until the Scot made his presence felt to Jeanie. Watching the man and girl go down, the *bandido* let out a snarl. However, he started to thrust himself up and saw the Kid running towards him. Maybe he could take the strangely-dressed man and the girl hostage, but not the *Cabrito* coming his way. Jerking up his revolver, the *bandido* cut loose a fast shot in the Kid's direction.

Flinging himself aside, the Kid missed death by inches. He went down in a rolling dive, landing on his stomach and throwing lead. Under the circumstances there was no time for fancy, careful shooting. A man could only get off his bullets as fast as possible in his enemy's general direction and hope that *Ka-Dih** would look with favour on his efforts.

Using the heel of his left hand to strike back the Dragoon's hammer, the Kid fanned off three very fast shots. Luck, or *Ka-Dih*, was with him. All three bullets hit their mark, ranging across from the *bandido's* right hip to the centre of his left breast. Lifted almost on to his feet by the impact of the bullets, the man threw his gun aside, spun around and pitched forward on to his face.

The last shooting, so close to them, proved the breaking point for the already spooked horses. Rearing and plunging, they scattered and went racing away. Although the Kid rose fast, he saw there would

**Ka-Dih:* The Great Spirit God of the Comanche.

be no hope of catching any of the fleeing animals. Even the one with the buckshot wound was running at speed and showed no sign of stopping.

Growling a curse, the Kid looked at the two *bandidos.* A man could only trust their kind after they were dead. By all appearances, the pair before him classed as trustworthy. Then he turned his eyes to where Jeanie's legs were flailing wildly from under Colin's body.

'Lemme go!' she yelled in a muffled voice. 'Take your stinking paws off me.'

'Best let her up afore she bites her way out through you, friend,' the Kid advised, walking to Colin's side and returning the Dragoon to its holster.

Kneeling up, the Scot looked at the Kid. Jeanie wriggled on to her back. Up until then she had thought that one of the *bandidos* was holding her. Instead she found it was the damned dude in the skirt that had brought her down. Glaring around, she saw the badly-needed horses racing away.

'Get yourself offen me, you *loco* son-of-a-bitch!' she spat furiously. 'What in hell game're you pulling? We needed those hosses!'

'Needed the ho——' Colin began and rose hurriedly, bending to offer her his hand. 'But I thought that you——'

Instinctively he knew that carrying on with his reason for stopping her would only make matters worse.

'You thought I was what?' Jeanie demanded, taking his hand and letting him draw her erect. 'Damn it, if you hadn't stopped me——'

'That *pelados** there would have,' the Kid put in. 'He was playing possum, gal, waiting to grab you.'

Jeanie looked at the body of the Kid's victim and nodded. Put that way, she could appreciate the danger so narrowly averted. However, she felt that Colin's motives sprang from a different, less complimentary reason. Rubbing her right hip, she scowled at the Scot.

**Pelados:* a corpse-robber or thief of the lowest kind.

'You near on bust me in half,' she complained. 'And the hosses're gone.'

'I can't tell you how sorry I am, miss,' Colin answered.

'Standing here whittle-whanging about it won't help,' Jeanie sniffed. 'I'll go see if Lou Temple needs help with the team.'

Watching the girl stalk away, Colin sucked in a deep breath. Admiration mingled with the worry lines on his face as he turned back to the Kid.

'Yon's a brave wee lassie. Most girls I've known would be screaming and swooning after what she's been through.'

'Jeanie was born and raised out here,' the Kid replied. 'She was fighting Indians when she was ten. This's not the first time she's been in a shoot-out.'

'It's my first time,' Colin said. 'I killed that man.'

'He'd've done as much for you——' the Kid began.

'What will the police say when they hear about it?' Colin interrupted.

'Davis' stinking State Police don't get out this way,' the Kid replied. 'Most any other lawman out here'll want to shake you by the hand. Only, if you've any sense, you'll not stop in Texas long enough for them to do it.'

'I don't understand you.'

'Feller you killed's called Adán Flores. His three brothers're going to come looking for you.'

'It was an accident,' Colin protested, guessing what the Kid meant by the cryptic words. 'His pistol went off when I knocked it up. I didn't mean for it to happen——'

'That won't make no never-mind to his brothers,' warned the Kid. 'All they'll know is that Adán's dead and they'll come gunning for whoever did it. Can you handle a gun?'

'I've used a rifle and a shotgun since I was a lad. But I'm not much of a hand with a pistol.'

'Best get that Spencer there unless you've a rifle along,' the Kid suggested. 'If the rest of 'em're around, you'll need one. How're you with that knife you're toting?'

'My dirk?' Colin replied, touching the hilt of the knife sheathed at his side. 'I've been taught to use it. But surely if I explained and——'

'They'll not give you time to explain,' the Kid growled. 'I know their kind. Do you want that rifle?'

'I've my own on the coach,' Colin answered, impressed by the seriousness with which the Kid spoke.

'Let's go unpack it then,' the young Texan ordered. 'Sooner we're moving, the better for all of us.'

Raising no more arguments, Colin walked at the Kid's side towards the trail. Jeanie was helping Temple to unhitch the dead horse and April leaned against the side of the coach struggling to control the nausea which welled inside her.

'Abel's a goner, Kid,' Temple said, straightening up.

'We'll load him on top and pull out as soon as you've give this gent his rifle,' the Kid replied. 'Can those three crow-bait haul the stage to Sawyer?'

'Sure they can,' the driver snorted, bristling at the insult to his highly-prized team. 'We won't be able to make fast time though.'

'Know who it was jumped us, Lou?' the Kid inquired mildly.

'Can't say as I do. We never got inter-duced formal like. Acted like raw yearling stock. Who was they?'

'That's Adán Flores,' the Kid told him, jerking a thumb in the direction of the appropriate body.

'The hell you say!' Temple spat out and Jeanie threw a startled glance at the corpse, then to Colin. After looking around, the driver went on, 'None of 'em got away, did they?'

'No. But their hosses lit out. We'd best get ready to move.'

'And *pronto*,' Jeanie put in, joining the men. 'I'll borrow the scatter, Lou.'

'Sure,' the driver replied. 'Come on, mister. Let's dig out your rifle.'

Going to the rear boot, Temple unfastened its cover and pulled out a long mahogany box. Colin unlocked and raised the lid. Inside it lay what looked like two twin-barrelled shotguns, a Henry rifle, a powder flask, two leather bullet pouches and four boxes of .44 cartridges for use with the repeater. Taking out the Henry and a box of cartridges, Colin relocked and replaced the box. While waiting, Temple kept scanning the surrounding country with worried eyes. The driver did not hide his relief when the box was replaced and the cover secured. Between them, the man wrapped Simcock's body in a spare boot cover, lifted it on to the roof and fastened it there.

'How about the other bodies?' Colin inquired when Temple sat on the driver's seat.

'We've only three hosses to haul the stage,' the Kid pointed out. 'That much extra weight'd kill them afore we've made three miles. The army or law'll come out to collect them.'

'You'd best stop up here, Kid,' Temple suggested.

'I figured to,' the Kid replied, 'Hand up my rifle, Jeanie-gal. Then all you get aboard, we're moving.'

Turkey vultures gathered in the sky, circling the scene of the abortive hold-up. Almost two hours had passed since the stagecoach continued its interrupted journey, but so far none of the black-winged scavengers had gathered sufficient courage to descend and begin their grisly work.

Topping a rim to the east, a rider reined in his horse at the sight of the hovering birds. From them, he dropped his gaze to the stage trail. For a moment he sat and stared, then turned in his saddle. Taking off his sombrero, he waved it over his head in a signal.

A few minutes went by and more men joined him. Then they urged their horses towards where the bodies lay. Twenty in number, they were well-armed, savage-looking Mexicans. Though most of them dressed after the fashion of *vaqueros*, nobody who knew the Rio Grande border country would have taken them for cattle-herders from a *hacienda*.

Best mounted of the party, and with a greater concern over what they saw, the Flores brothers drew ahead of their men. Riding in a shallow V formation, the brothers glared about them with all the caution of much-hunted *lobo* wolves. If the bodies had been left to lure them into a trap, they intended to locate it before it could spring on them.

As usual, Tiburcio formed the point of the V. Tall, swarthily handsome and slim, he gave the impression of rapier-steel strength. Although travel-stained, his clothing had the look of costly elegance. Silver glinted in the band of his white sombrero, decorated his short brown leather jacket, saddle and bridle. Around his waist hung a gunbelt of shining black leather, supporting an 1860 Army Colt with fancy Tiffany grips in a fast-draw holster on the right and a long-bladed fighting knife at the left. He could use either weapon with considerable skill. Sitting his black and white *tobiano* stallion with easy grace, he studied the scene ahead with cold, calculating intensity.

To Tiburcio's left rode Vicente. Youngest of the brothers, he dressed as stylishly as any rich *haciendero's* favourite son. Lines of dissipation and evil already marred his handsome features, hinting at the true, merciless nature underneath. Silver sparkled on his clothing, horse's rig and traced patterns on the ivory handles of the two Navy Colts riding butt forward in the holsters of his gunbelt. His *bayo naranjado** gelding moved gracefully, if nervously, for he used spurs, quirt and ring bit impartially to enforce his will.

If his brothers might have passed for high-born Spanish Mexicans, the same did not apply to Matteo. Middle-sized, thickset, he had a face which even a mother would find hard to love. A jagged knife-scar down the left cheek did nothing to improve the effect of a receding forehead, sunken eyes, a crooked nose

**Bayo naranjado:* a bright orange dun with white mane and tail.

and thick, surly lips. He had a scarlet bandana bound about his head and his sombrero trailed by its storm-strap on his back. A filthy white shirt hung open to show a hair-matted chest. Dirty white pantaloons covered his lower regions and bare feet rested in the stirrups of an Indian saddle. Only the Dragoon Colt in an open-bottomed half-breed holster and heavy, long-bladed *machete* hanging from the other side of his weapon belt showed any sign of care or cleaning. He slouched afork a runty buckskin that looked like it was waiting for the turkey vultures to feed on it and could out-run any horse in the gang.

'It looks as if Brother Adán tried to rob a stagecoach,' Vicente commented. 'And did as well at it as at every——'

'Shut your mouth and use your eyes!' Tiburcio barked, head turning from side to side as he searched for any hint of danger. 'What do you think, Matteo?'

Before answering, Matteo looked up at the vultures and then examined the land around the bodies. Knowing his brother's thoroughness and ability in such matters, Tiburcio was content to wait for an answer.

'There's nobody around,' Matteo decided.

'The birds haven't come down to feed yet,' Tiburcio pointed out, although willing to accept the verdict.

'Maybe whoever he tried to rob have only just gone,' Matteo answered. 'Indians might be able to hide around there without me seeing them, but no white man could.'

Satisfied that there was no danger of them riding into an ambush, Tiburcio kept moving. However, he did not go straight to the bodies, but led his party on to the trail some distance from where they lay. He wanted to learn how Adán came to be killed. So he kept the horses away from where they might trample over tracks or other signs that would tell so much to trained eyes. Although there was no immediate threat, he did not forget to take the basic precautions against being surprised.

'Two of you go each way and watch the trail,' he barked, halting the *tobiano* and dismounting.

While two of the gang rode off in each direction, Matteo and Vicente swung from their saddles. Leaving their horses standing 'ground hitched' with trailing reins, the brothers walked forward. Without as much as glancing at the other bodies, they approached Adán. Matteo's eyes raked across the ground, noticing every bent-over blade of grass and reading its message. So did Tiburcio and a puzzled frown crept on to his face.

Going to the body, Matteo knelt by it and turned the head to look at the wound. A perplexed expression creased his face and he made the sign of the cross as he studied the burning caused by the muzzle-blast.

'How could it happen?' Matteo breathed.

'Adán was always stupid——' Vicente answered.

'Not stupid enough to let a man walk up and put a gun against the side of his head,' Matteo interrupted.

'His gun's been fired,' Tiburcio went on, having picked up the Starr and checked its condition. 'There's no sign that he hit anything.'

While the brothers devoted their attention to Adán, the rest of the gang fanned out to examine the other bodies. Enough of them could read-sign and tell roughly what had happened. However, their main concern was to search the corpses, not to worry over why the robbery had gone wrong. One of the men reached the side of Temple's victim and made a discovery.

'*Patron!*' he yelled. 'Arturo's alive!'

Thrusting the Starr into his waistband, Tiburcio strode rapidly towards the speaker. His haste sprang from a desire for information rather than interest in the wounded man's welfare.

Pain from the hoof-graze had combined with the two buckshot wounds to render Arturo unconscious. In his hurry to leave before the rest of the gang arrived, the Kid had not made a close examination of the shot *bandidos*. So the fact that Arturo lived had gone undiscovered. During the time Arturo had lain insensible, the wounds continued to bleed. So he regained consciousness too weak to do more than lie and make feeble movements which prevented the cautious vultures from landing. Shortly before the gang appeared, he had fainted again.

'Bring water and *tequila*!' Tiburcio called to the men by the trail, looking down at Arturo's haggard features. 'Move yourselves, or somebody will wish he had.'

Gathering around, the rest of the gang watched as Tiburcio splashed water on to Arturo's face and poured *tequila* into his mouth. After a short time Arturo's eyes opened and he looked around in a puzzled manner. Instantly the men standing around him started to ask questions.

'Who killed Jaime?' one demanded.

'What went wrong?' asked another.

'How——' began a third.

'Silence!' Tiburcio roared, glaring furiously at the speakers. Then he remembered the first of them was Jaime's brother. 'Stay here, Manuel. The rest of you collect the weapons and load Adán—and Jaime—on to horses.'

Every member of the gang learned real early to obey orders without question or hesitation. So they slunk away like children from an irascible schoolteacher, to carry out their leader's command. Only Manuel remained with the brothers, his face impassive but his stocky frame quivering with rage and grief.

'Water!' Arturo croaked, recognition coming to his face.

'What happened?' Matteo inquired after giving the wounded man a drink.

'We saw a stagecoach and Adán said we should rob it,' Arturo croaked. 'There was shooting——'

'I can see that!' Tiburcio spat out. 'Who killed Adán?'

'It was a man dressed in a skirt,' Arturo replied and saw disbelief on the listener's faces. 'It is true. I swear it by the Holy Mother. The man wore a skirt. Adán and Jaime laughed at him and Adán called him over and was going to look what he wore under the skirt. The man knocked Adán's gun up and there was a shot. Then *Cabrito*——'

'*Cabrito!*' Matteo snarled. 'Was that son of an Indian whore here.'

'He was on the stagecoach,' Arturo confirmed. 'He killed Indio and Luis——'

'Who killed Jaime?' Manuel put in.

'A woman——'

'Not the man dressed in a skirt?' Vicente sneered.

'No,' Arturo replied. 'My wounds, *patrón*. They must be bandaged.'

'We'll see to them,' Tiburcio promised. 'Just tell us all that happened first.'

Slowly Arturo gave the brothers an account of the hold-up and what had followed. He confirmed the story Matteo had read from the tracks and they saw how Adán had let himself be diverted, then killed.

'Just what you'd expect from him,' Vicente commented. 'Do we go after the coach and see this man-in-a-skirt?'

'Look at the horses,' Tiburcio told him. 'We'd run them into the ground trying to catch it.'

'There're only three horses pulling it,' Vicente protested, his wish for revenge activated more by blood-lust than grief over Adán's death.

'And they've a good two hours start,' Tiburcio told him. 'By the time we caught up, they'd be near to Fort Sawyer.'

'Fine fools we'd look killing them outside the town,' Matteo went on, 'then trying to out-run a posse on tired horses.'

'So what do we do?' Vicente demanded. 'Sit here and pray for Adán's soul while the man who killed him gets away?'

'Watch your mouth, little brother!' Tiburcio snarled. 'One fool of the family's already tried to think for himself today and look how it turned out.'

Cold fury showed on Vicente's face, but he knew

better than voice his objections to the comment. Knowing how much their power and safety depended on the fear the Flores' name inspired, Matteo threw a warning scowl at Vicente and turned his attention back to Tiburcio. None of them felt any real grief over Adán's death, but all knew that they would be expected to take revenge on the people involved in it. The difference between Matteo and Vicente was that the former realised his limitations and left the planning to Tiburcio.

'We're going after whoever killed Adán, aren't we?' Vicente asked, controlling his temper and speaking almost mildly.

'Of course we are,' Tiburcio agreed. 'But we do it *my* way. You'll go with half of the men and take the bodies to the San Patricio mission for burial. Then meet me on Onion Creek south of Fort Sawyer tomorrow.'

'If you say so,' Vicente muttered sullenly, after a brief pause.

'I say so. We won't make a move until you come,' Tiburcio replied, then turned his attention towards Manuel who was hovering in the background. 'Go with Vicente, *amigo* and see your brother is buried as you would wish it.'

'*Si, patrón*,' the *bandido* answered. 'And when I come back, I will have the woman who killed him.'

'We'll know where to find her by then,' Tiburcio promised. 'When we get to the Creek, Matteo, we'll send a man into town to fetch Arnaldo Hogan out to us.'

'He'll know all there is to know,' Matteo agreed. 'Let's ride.'

'*Patrón!*' Arturo gasped, watching the brothers turn away. 'What about my wounds?'

'See to them for him Vicente,' Tiburcio ordered.

For once the youngest brother accepted an order without question or hesitation. Drawing and cocking his right-hand Colt, he swung back towards the wounded man. Neither Tiburcio nor Matteo looked back as the shot cracked out. Walking over to the waiting men, Tiburcio told them what he wanted done. Vicente joined his brothers, holstering the smoking Colt.

'His wounds don't trouble him now,' the youngster said.

'Let's ride.' His eyes met those of Manuel and he went on. 'The sooner we've done this, the sooner we can get our revenge.'

Chapter Four

Colin Farquharson was a worried, puzzled man as he left his room at the Grand Hotel to go downstairs for a meal. Born and raised in the Scottish highlands, he found difficulty in understanding the casual manner in which the law enforcement officer in Fort Sawyer reacted to hearing of the attempted armed robbery and killing of five men.

Once the stagecoach had started moving with its depleted team, Colin found himself with time to think. He began to wonder what would happen when the local police, or whatever they might be, learned that he had killed a man.

Seeing that he was concerned, April had set about diverting him. With the deft ease of a professional hostess, she got him talking. Remarking that she had left Galveston to take a better job in a Fort Sawyer saloon, she inquired what brought Colin to Texas. Only too pleased to have his thoughts taken from the killing, he told her how his uncle had been a major in the Confederate States cavalry and had spoken in such glowing terms on his return to Scotland that Colin had decided to see the Lone Star State for himself. A cousin lived in Fort Sawyer, so Colin planned to visit him before starting on a hunting expedition.

For her part, Jeanie had made it plain that she did not want to join in the conversation. Nursing the dead guard's shotgun, she had answered the few questions directed at her in monosyllables and showed that she wished to be left alone. Colin had put the girl's reticence down to annoyance at how he had treated her, while April regarded it as no more than a 'good' woman's snobbish objections to travelling with a saloonworker. As long as daylight lasted, Jeanie had repeatedly leaned out of the window and looked back along the trail. She showed considerable relief when the Ysabel Kid called from the roof that the lights of the town were in sight.

Night had fallen as the coach passed through the Mexican section, went along the main street and came to a halt before the stage depot. Although Colin's appearance had attracted some comment among the crowd awaiting the coach's arrival, news of what had delayed it took their attention from him.

On his arrival the county sheriff had asked questions, most of which the Kid and Temple answered. Much to Colin's surprise, the paunchy, miserable-looking peace officer accepted all he was told and did not offer to take down written statements. He had expressed satisfaction on hearing of Adán Flores' death and stated that Colin did not need to worry about the other brothers seeking revenge while staying in Fort Sawyer; a comment which brought a low grunt of disapproval from the Kid. Promising that he would take out a posse to collect the bodies in the morning, the sheriff told the passengers that they could go about their business.

After repeating his warning that Colin should watch out for the remaining Flores brothers, the Kid collected his saddle and disappeared along the street in the direction of the army post. For a moment Jeanie had stood staring at Colin, seeming on the verge of speaking. Then she turned and walked away in the opposite direction to that taken by the Kid. After reminding Colin to come over for a drink later, April had crossed the street and entered the Black Bear Saloon.

Asking the depot agent about his cousin, Colin had learned that Tam Breda was away on business and not expected back for some weeks. Further questioning brought the information that the Grand

Hotel was the best hotel in town. A small, sly-looking, dirty man called Arnie had offered to help carry his baggage to the hotel. On the way, Arnie had asked many questions about the hold-up which Colin put down to idle morbid curiosity.

Despite its grandiloquent title, the Grand Hotel proved to be a two-floor wooden building of no great size. If lacking in many of the facilities Colin expected in a hotel, it was clean and he had decided it would suit his purpose until Breda returned.

Walking down the stairs, Colin saw a tall, lean young man studying him from the reception desk. Straightening up, the young man ambled across the room. He had reddish-brown hair and a cheery, freckled face. A battered Confederate Army forage cap perched on his head and he wore a buckskin shirt, levis pants and riding boots. Although his face had an amiable grin, he kept his right hand thumb-hooked into his gunbelt close to the butt of a long-barrelled Army Colt.

'Howdy,' the man greeted, freeing his thumb and extending the hand in Colin's direction. 'Name's Kenny Schell. My lil sister, Jeanie, told me what happened on the trail. So I figured least I could do was come around and thank you for saving her hide.'

'I didn't save her,' Colin objected, shaking hands.

'That's how she tells it,' Kenny replied. 'If that greaser'd laid hands on her, she'd be dead—or wishing she was—right now.'

'The cowboy shot the man,' Colin insisted. 'All I did was stop your sister catching one of the horses.'

'She told me how you stopped her,' Kenny chuckled, 'I'd vote Republican to've seed her face when you hauled her down. Happen you're not ag'in it. I'd sure admire to buy you a drink.'

Suddenly Colin felt the need for company. He also decided that a second meeting with Jeanie Schell might be interesting, especially as she appeared to have lost her animosity towards him. There was something friendly and appealing about Kenny which suggested he might be worth cultivating as a companion. So Colin smiled and indicated the dining room.

'I'm just going in to eat. Will you join me?'

'Be right pleased to,' Kenny grinned. 'We could go home for some victuals, but Ma 'n' Jeanie's out visiting.'

If Colin had been more experienced in western ways, he might have read significance in the way Kenny acted. After shaking hands, the young Texan returned his thumb to the belt. While walking towards the dining room, Kenny's eyes darted from side to side. He was tense, watchful and, to anyone who knew of such things, ready for trouble. Leading the way into the room, Kenny gave its few occupants a quick scrutiny. Then he walked by the empty tables in the centre of the room, selecting one against the wall and not in direct line with either door or windows.

Hanging his hat on the back of the chair, Kenny sat down and looked his companion over. Colin was still bare-headed, and had left off his plaid and the dirk.

'Don't you have a gun, Colin?' Kenny inquired, after the Scot introduced himself.

'I've a Henry, a shotgun and a double-barrelled rifle.'

'No handgun?'

'No. I've a brace of pistols——'

'Why aren't you packing 'em?' Kenny asked bluntly.

'I didn't see any need to go armed in town,' Colin replied.

The young Texan let out his breath in a long hiss. 'That was Adán Flores you killed on the trail. Didn't the Kid warn you that his kin'd be gunning for you?'

'Yes. But the sheriff said I'd have nothing to worry about in town.'

'Henny Lansing don't know a greaser from a Tejas Injun,' Kenny scoffed. 'You should've listened to the Kid. Now there's a feller who *knows* Mexicans. Will you be staying around for long?'

'Until Tam Breda comes back,' Colin answered.

'That long, huh?' Kenny said. 'I can't sti——'

At that moment the waiter arrived, a gnarled old-timer who rattled off a string of unintelligible names instead of offering a printed menu. So Colin took the easy way out.

'What do you suggest, Kenny?'

'Son-of-a-bitch stew, followed by apple pie,' the Texan answered.

'I respect your judgement,' Colin said as the waiter hobbled away. 'But what was that you ordered?'

'Son-of-a-bitch stew?' Kenny grinned. 'It's made out of most of a calf, 'cepting the hide, hooves and bellow, potatoes, stuff like that, cut up small and stewed up until you can't tell which son-of-a-bitching part's which.'

Despite the description, Colin found the stew very appetising. While eating, he turned the conversation to the Schell family. From what Kenny said, they lived a nomadic life, catching wild horses, and had come to Fort Sawyer hoping to obtain a contract to supply remounts for the Army.

'We should get it,' Kenny continued as they finished the meal. 'Pappy taught us all he knew about mustanging and we've a good crew of men.'

'I wish you every success then,' Colin stated, shoving back his chair. 'And now for that drink. Miss Hosman, she was on the coach with us, invited me to the Black Bear Saloon. Shall we try there?'

'It's the best place in town,' Kenny replied.

'Your sister didn't mention why she was travelling,' Colin remarked as they walked out of the dining room.

'Went to Brownsville to see some of our kin,' Kenny answered, and for a moment a cold, worried expression flickered across his face. 'Do you want to go up and fetch your gun?'

'Surely not just to walk along the street,' Colin protested.

'Have it your way,' Kenny drawled. 'Only don't

count on getting up close to any more of the Flores boys. They'll shoot you on sight.'

Although Colin thought that Kenny was exaggerating the danger, he kept quiet. To a man reared in the British Isles, it seemed improbable that known outlaws would dare to come into a town on a mission of revenge. So he declined to fetch the pistols from his room. Giving a resigned shrug, Kenny took the lead as they left the hotel.

Once the train of thought had been started, Colin could not help noticing the caution Kenny displayed. Before letting Colin through the door, Kenny swept the street in each direction with a cautious gaze. The young Texan spoke little and remained alert as they crossed the street and approached the Black Bear Saloon. Even as Colin began to wonder why the other had chosen to stay in his company, they reached the batwing doors at the front entrance.

Before offering to open the doors, Kenny looked the room's occupants over. He saw only the usual sort of crowd, a few soldiers, townsmen, a sprinkling of range-country dwellers, waiters and half-a-dozen garishly-dressed girls. There were no Mexicans present in the bar or on the balcony leading to the upstairs rooms.

Colin became the target for every eye as he entered. Although he saw various customers clearly talking about him, none of them came over or addressed him.

'They're telling each other about you killing Adán Flores,' Kenny remarked as he and Colin approached the bar.

'Do they know about it?' the Scot asked.

'Everybody in town will by now,' Kenny replied. 'Likely they're wondering how soon it'll be afore Tiburcio Flores comes after you. What'll you have?'

'Whisky,' Colin answered, looking around the room then turning to the bartender who came they way. 'Is Miss Hosman here?'

'You're the feller who killed Adán Flores, huh?'

the man asked, looking nervously around the room. 'Sure, she's here.' He nodded towards the stairs at the side of the room. 'I'll send word up to her that you've come.'

Following the direction of the bartender's gaze, Colin saw a sharp-featured, middle-sized, scrawny man on the stairs. Dressed in dirty range clothes, with a Navy Colt holstered on his hip, the man stared towards the bar. Yet Colin got the idea that, for once, he was not the object of interest. Seeing Colin and Kenny looking his way, the man turned and slouched back to disappear on to the balcony.

'How long's Sprig Branch been in town, barkeep?' Kenny asked.

'Who?' the bartender grunted as he took up a bottle of whisky.

'That feller on the stairs didn't come in on his lonesome,' Kenny stated.

'Him and three pards come in just after sundown,' the bartender explained, pouring drinks into glasses. 'Miss Hosman said for you to have the first one on her, mister.'

'I'm getting to like her afore I meet her,' Kenny grinned, finding himself included in the gift. 'Here's long life to you and her, Colin.'

'And to you,' Colin answered, raising his glass. The drink had a raw bite to it and did not taste like the whisky distilled in his native Highlands, but was better than he expected. 'I take it you knew yon wee feller who was looking us over from the stairs.'

'Sure,' Kenny agreed. 'It's Slinky Moore, works with Sprig Branch. They're *mesteneros*, mustangers.'

'Like you.'

'I wouldn't thank you for thinking it. Mustanging's a rough game, but I'd sooner vote Republican than handle hosses the way Branch and his bunch do.'

'How do you mean?' Colin asked.

'I don't go much on a feller who uses clogs, or drag chains on the hosses he catches,' Kenny replied. 'Branch's bunch do that—and worse. I was right,

Slinky ain't here on his lonesome.'

Turning his head slightly, Colin saw four men coming down the stairs. Two of them were gangling, unshaven, with hatchet faces, wearing buckskins, moccasins and with knives as well as revolvers slung about them. Kenny whispered that they were Sam and Eric Trimble.

Sprig Branch topped the Trimbles by maybe an inch, being around six foot tall and heavy-built. Black hair straggled untidily from beneath his dirty Jeff Davis campaign hat and stubbled his surly face. He had on a grey shirt, riding breeches of faded blue and calf-high Indian moccasins. Butt forward on an Army weapon belt hung a Remington revolver. Like his companions, he showed signs of long, hard riding.

'Howdy, Kenny,' Branch greeted, coming to the bar followed by his men. 'Didn't figure on finding you here. How's Ma and lil Jeanie?'

'Well enough,' Kenny replied, watching the men fan in a half circle around him and Colin. 'You all right, Sprig?'

'Nothing wrong with me that getting an Army remount contract won't cure,' Branch answered and hooked his elbow on the counter. 'Which same's's good's got.'

'Nice to be sure,' Kenny said dryly, turning with his back to the bar and facing the Trimble brothers. Moore stood beyond Colin, a sly, vicious grin twisting his lips.

'There's nobody else for it,' Branch stated.

' 'Cepting me,' Kenny commented.

'Your pard sure dresses elegant, Kenny,' Eric Trimble remarked. 'I ain't never seed a feller wearing a skirt afore.'

'Now that ain't the truth, lil brother,' Sam Trimble put in. 'We did so see one. Back in Galveston afore the War. Only he wore a wig, face-paint and jewellery as well. Them sailor-boys sure used to come 'round him like bees to honey.'

Sucking in his breath, Colin put down the glass. He still faced the bar, but could see the Trimbles' leering faces reflected in the mirror. Something about them gave Colin a warning. The two men were looking for trouble, that showed in their attitude. Not wanting to become involved in a brawl, Colin tightened his lips and ignored the words. A red flush crept up the back of his neck and he clenched his fists.

'I mind the feller,' Eric continued. 'They say he used to dress like a gal all the way through. Fancy frilly drawers and all. Is that what you wear, feller—or should I say "girlie"?'

Still Colin refused to be goaded. However, Kenny looked at Branch and growled, 'Call 'em off, Sprig.'

'The boys're only funning, Kenny,' Branch answered in a carrying tone, but made no attempt to do as the young mustanger asked.

'I asked you a question, girlie,' Eric said. 'What do you wear under that skirt?'

Slowly Colin turned to face his tormentors. 'I'm thinking you'd best mind your own business.'

Games stopped and conversation around the room drifted to an end as the people present became aware that the group at the bar were doing more than making idle conversation. Moving along the sober side of the counter, the bartender hoped to prevent trouble.

'Take it easy, boys,' he said in a placating manner. 'Let's all have a drink and keep things friendly.'

'Sure we will,' Sam agreed. 'Only if we're all so friendly, this feller oughta show us what's under his skirt.'

Watching the others, Branch grinned. On learning of Kenny Schell's presence, he had seen a way to remove his only rival for the Army remount contract. No other mustangers were in the area and the Army needed horses badly. So their buying commission would award the contract to the first *mesteneros* who applied. All too well Branch knew the Schell family's reputation and so did the Army. Even with Trader dead, the soldiers might figure the Schells their best bet. However, if Kenny met with an accident there was no other man to take his place.

From Moore's description, Branch had guessed

Colin's nationality and figured how the Scot would react to comments about his kilt. So he had given orders for his men to pick on Colin. That way it would seem the trouble started with the Scot and Kenny became involved by accident. Once a fight began, it would be easy to see that Kenny did not walk away from it.

Aware of what his boss wanted, Moore winked at the Trimbles and took hold of the kilt's hem.

'Let's take a loo——,' the little man began.

And got no further with words or actions. Letting out a low growl, Colin laid his left hand on Moore's face and pushed. Lifted from his feet, the small man went reeling down the bar, tripped over a spittoon and sat on his rump with some force.

Realising that there was no hope of avoiding trouble, Colin wisely decided to make the best of it. He had no intention of giving up his national dress, so figured an example of his fighting skill might cool off other such incidents.

A startled curse broke from Sam Trimble and he began to turn on Colin. Swinging around from pushing Moore, the Scot crashed a backhand blow which caught the side of Sam's jaw and pitched him headlong into his brother. With a snarl, Eric shoved Sam away—and almost immediately wished that he had not. Gliding in, Colin drove his right fist against Eric's stomach. Feeling as if he had been kicked in the stomach by a mule, Eric reeled back. His eyes bulged out, hands clasped at his mid-section and he dropped to his knees, moaning.

Branch gulped, backing away along the bar and staring as if mesmerised at the scene before him. Beyond Kenny and Colin, Moore sat looking dazed. Sam hung against a table, shaking his head in an attempt to control its tendency to spin. From all appearances, it would be some time before Eric felt like resuming hostilities. Sucking in a breath, Branch tried to put on an indignant front.

'There was no cause for that,' he growled. 'The boys were only funning.'

'They're not laughing any,' Kenny replied. 'You taking it up for them?'

Before Branch could reply, Sam moved from the table. Straightening up, he rubbed the back of his hand across his mouth, looked at the blood smeared on it and spat out a curse.

'You stinking swish!*' Sam snarled, spreading his fingers over the butt of his Colt. 'Fill your hand!'

'He's not wearing a gun,' Kenny put in, watching Eric lurch erect and Moore stand then move to Sam's side.

'Then he's going to hoist up that skirt and show us what's under it!' Eric gritted, joining his brother.

'How's about it, Branch?' Kenny asked, not taking his eyes from the trio. 'Are you letting them take this through?'

'You know how it is now you're one, Kenny,' Branch answered as he ranged himself alongside Eric. 'A boss has to stand by his men.'

'So that's the way it is, huh?' Kenny said quietly. 'If it's me you're after, say so and let Colin go.'

'We're not after anybody, Kenny,' Branch stated, raising his voice to carry around the room. 'Only that feller jumped my boys and we don't reckon it's right. So we aim to do what we started out to do.'

Colin listened, only partly understanding what was going on. Inexperienced though he was, he read the menace in the four men's attitude. Suddenly he realised that the affair had gone beyond mere horse-play. Yet no Scot would tamely submit to the indignity the quartet tried to force on him. Colin knew that if he stayed on, there would be bad trouble.

'I think we'd better leave,' he said to Kenny.

'Not without doing what we said,' Eric growled.

'We're coming through,' Kenny announced and the listening crowd prepared to take cover.

'The hell you are!' Sam snarled.

'Through or over,' Kenny warned. 'Let's go, Colin.'

**Swish:* a homosexual.

Chapter Five

With a sigh of relief, Jeanie Schell fastened the buckle of her waistbelt and wriggled her body in near ecstasy. On the bed lay her dress and the sun bonnet, discarded along with the high-button shoes at the first opportunity. Her short, curly hair was no longer hidden and she wore the kind of clothes the Kid remembered as her normal outfit: a boy's tartan shirt and levis pants with their cuffs hanging cowhand style outside high heeled riding boots. Giving another sigh of satisfaction, she walked out of the bedroom.

Following their custom where possible, the Schell family were living in a cabin left deserted by its previous owner. Long used to such temporary homes, Ma had settled them in comfortably. In the two days since she and Kenny arrived, she had cleaned up the cabin and augmented the furniture left by the departed owner with items of her own carried in their wagon. The result was that they had a house for their stay in Fort Sawyer, furnished adequately if not luxuriously. Ma had lived all her married life under similar conditions and accepted them as payment for a very happy marriage.

Of middle height, Ma might easily have been taken for Jeanie's elder sister. She had married young and carried her thirty-nine years well. Blonde hair as short and curly as her daughter's framed a merry, pretty face. Ma's buxom figure was squeezed into unaccustomed corsets and a sober black dress suitable for going town-visiting. Like Jeanie, she did not care for such clothing; which accounted, more than any other reason, for the disapproving manner in which she eyed her daughter.

Sensing an attack on her choice of clothes was imminent, and aware of what caused it, Jeanie tried to divert it.

'We've enough on our hands right now without Kenny having to wet-nurse that Scotch feller, Ma,' she said.

'He saved you,' Ma replied. 'We're beholden to him for that.'

'The Kid saved me as well, comes to that,' Jeanie protested, wanting to keep the conversation going long enough for her mother to forget the irritation of the corsets. 'Aren't we beholden to him too?'

'If the Ysabel Kid don't know how to look out for his-self by now, he's been living on luck since he was ten,' Ma answered. 'The Kid knows Mexicans like your pappy knew mustanging. That Scotch boy doesn't know 'em, so I figure we owe him some help.'

As she mentioned her husband, Ma turned her eyes towards the fireplace. Following the direction of her mother's gaze, Jeanie knew what attracted Ma's attention. Hung in a place of honour on the wall above the fireplace was an ivory handled Dragoon Colt. It had been her father's gun and looking at it reminded Jeanie afresh of her family's financial situation.

Times were hard in Texas. Although not a slave-owning State, except on a very limited scale, its pre-War Administration had elected to secede from the Union. The South lost the War and Texans worked to rebuild their State. In one way they might have counted themselves lucky. Texas' vast distances and small Negro population prevented the heavy hand of Reconstruction falling on any but the more civilised eastern and northern areas. In the south and west life went on much as before the War, but defeat brought problems in its wake.

Produced to replace the Union's monetary system, the currency of the Confederate States became valueless paper with the North's victory. Which meant that the people of Texas had to start almost from scratch if they hoped to re-establish their shattered economy. The State had no conventional industries capable of competing for business on a nation-wide level, but it possessed a rich natural wealth that might possibly be developed.

Chief source of natural wealth was cattle. Left all but untended through the years of the War, the herds of longhorns had multiplied practically unchecked. They offered a potential way to solvency which a few far-seeing men could understand. However, the way back to financial stability would not be easy. Two major problems needed solving. Where to sell the stock and how to handle the half-wild cattle on the great, unfenced Texas range country.

The second problem was of most interest to the Schell family. To work cattle, men needed horses. During the War, the Confederate States Army drew remounts in plenty from the Texas ranchers. To tend and round up their cattle, they had to rebuild their remudas. That was where mustangers like the Schell family came in. Mustangs roamed in great numbers in certain sections of the range country, untamed but offering the answer to the ranchers' needs. Under the rugged, merciless laws of nature only the fittest horses survived; animals used to fending for themselves and able to keep in good health on what they could forage. So the wild horses became a vital necessity to the recovery of Texas.

Gathering mustangs was not so easy as the uninitiated might believe. Men like Trader Schell had long made it their profession. They knew where to look for the greatest concentrations, developing techniques to catch and hold together large numbers of wild horses. With their superior skill, the professional mustangers could supply a rancher's needs in less time and cheaper than he might using his own men.

Although there was a steady demand for horses, Trader Schell had not grown rich. Only a few ranchers, those who had been wise enough to convert some of their money into gold during the War, could pay cash for the stock. The rest traded property to fill their needs, or gave notes-of-hand for cattle in exchange for the horses. Despite cattle still having little more than hide-and-tallow value, knowing the ranchers' desperate position, Trader had accepted the notes. He still had to meet his overheads and storekeepers fought shy of taking anything but money.

After Trader's death, the family had decided to continue mustanging. It was the only business they knew. One of the main reasons for the decision had been the news, passed on by a friend in a position to know, that the Army wanted remounts for its forthcoming campaigns against the hostile Indians. Such a chance could not be ignored. The Army paid well—and in cash—for its horses. According to the friend's information, the Army needed a large number of horses and would look favourably on Trader Schell supplying them as he had a reputation for honesty and producing animals in good condition.

The only trouble was that Trader had been killed before the letter arrived. However, Ma felt sure that the family could carry on. They knew the mustanging business thoroughly, having been well taught by her husband. Money would be their chief difficulty. Paying off their *mesteneros* did not leave enough cash to buy the supplies needed for an extensive hunt. Much against her will, Ma had decided to ask her husband's brother for help. Trader had set the man up in business before the war and Ma sent Jeanie to Brownsville to explain the situation.

Thinking of how the trip had turned out, the girl made a wry face.

'Damn Uncle Jabez!' she spat out, taking her eyes from the old Dragoon. 'He could've helped us out. He allowed he couldn't hardly make ends meet; and there was Cousin Annie-Jo all dressed up in a fancy silk frock, with a cupboard full of 'em.'

'I never did cotton to Jabez,' Ma admitted. 'Only I figured he'd see his way to help out for a share of the profits, if not because Trader was his only brother.'

'Some folk forget real easy,' Jeanie said bitterly.

If the Ysabel Kid had been on hand to hear the words, he would have understood the girl's behaviour on the stagecoach. In his life Trader Schell had been generous, especially to his brother. Yet Jabez Schell had not been able to see his way clear to help out his sister-in-law and her family, despite the fact that his business was running successfully. A good-hearted girl, with love and respect for her father, Jeanie deeply resented what she regarded as the treachery to his memory.

'We'll get by,' Ma stated. 'Even without Uncle Jabez's help.'

Since her return, Jeanie had found no time to catch up on the local developments. First she had told of the hold up. Hearing of Colin's actions, Ma had decided that Kenny should go and guard the young Scot against reprisals by the Flores brothers. A bath followed, then Jeanie put on her usual style of clothing. So she had not yet found an opportunity to ask about their future plans.

'What'll we do now, Ma?' she asked.

'Like we come to do,' Ma answered. 'Go and see the Army's hoss buyer at noon tomorrow and try for the contract.'

'How about the supplies we need to go out again?'

'Dick Hoffer'll stake us if we get the contract.'

A knock on the front door prevented the discussion being extended. Nodding to her daughter, Ma went to pick up the Sharps carbine which leaned against the side of the fireplace. With the click of the Sharps' hammer coming to full cock following her, Jeanie crossed the room.

'Who-all's out there?' she called.

'Dusty Fog,' a familiar voice replied.

Letting out a sigh, Ma lowered the carbine and set its hammer down again. Jeanie opened the door without hesitation. In addition to being a friend of long standing, the man outside was something of a legend in his own young life-time.

During the War, his age no more than seventeen years, Dusty Fog held rank as captain in the Texas Light Cavalry. To folk in his home State, and both sides on the Arkansas battlefront, his ability as a military raider had been rated above the more publicised Turner Ashby or John Singleton Mosby. His exploits included taking ten thousand dollars from a Yankee pay-master,* helping the equally legendary Rebel Spy to destroy a forging plant meant to flood the South with counterfeit money,† and wiping out Hannah's band of murderous renegades.‡

On his return to Texas, the crippling of Ole Devil Hardin—by a horse the Schells captured—put Dusty Fog as segundo of the great OD Connected ranch.§ He had recently returned from completing a mission of some importance in Mexico and was once more plunged into the business of rebuilding the ranch. Many tales were told of his courage, chivalry and ability. In addition to being lightning fast on the draw, he could shoot with considerable accuracy from either hand and stood second to no man when it came to rough-house brawling.

Two men stood on the porch, illuminated by the light from the open door. One was at least six foot three in height, a golden blond giant with an almost classically handsome face. In his right hand, he held a white Stetson, its band decorated by silver conchas. All his clothes, although functional and cowhand style, had been made to measure. A green silk bandana trailed over his tan-coloured shirt, the latter cut to set off his great spread of shoulders and tapering waist. Everything about him hinted at enormous strength. Around his middle hung a wide leather gunbelt, two ivory handled Army Colts in carefully designed holsters rode on it. Such a rig would allow very fast withdrawal of the guns.

Compared with his companion, the other man

* Told in *The Colt and the Sabre.*

†Told in the *Rebel Spy.*

‡Told in *The Bad Bunch.*

§Told in *The Fastest Gun in Texas.*

seemed hardly worth a second glance. From his curly dusty blond hair to the high-heeled boots on his feet he stood no more than five foot six. Good looking, it was not in the eye-catching way of the blond giant. Although his calfskin vest, blue shirt and levis pants were of the best quality, he contrived to make them look like somebody's cast-offs. Not even the excellently made gunbelt and twin bone-handled Army Colts riding butt forward in its holsters made the small man more noticeable. Yet, if one chose to look closely, there was a strength, intelligence and power in his face. The clothes concealed rather than revealed the small man's well-developed physique.

It was to the second man, the insignificant-seeming young cowhand, that Jeanie addressed her welcome.

'Come in, Cap'n Dusty. And you, friend.'

'Howdy, Jeanie, Ma,' Dusty Fog greeted, entering the cabin followed by his companion. 'This's Mark Counter.'

In the near future Mark Counter became known for his enormous strength and ability as a roughhouse fighter. His taste in clothes dictated what the well-dressed Texas cowhand would wear. However, that evening in Fort Sawyer neither Jeanie nor Ma had heard of him.

Son of a Big Bend rancher, Mark had joined Dusty and the Kid during the former's mission into Mexico. Instead of returning to his home when the mission ended, he decided to become a member of the OD Connected. Not just a ranch hand, but as one of the floating outfit; a small select group who travelled the back ranges, or handled work away from the spread.

'My pleasure, ma'am,' Mark said with old-time courtesy.

'We were real sorry to hear about Trader, Ma,' Dusty went on. 'Uncle Devil sends his respects.'

'Thank you, Dusty,' Ma replied. 'Rest your feet. Have you fed?'

'Colonel at the post gave us supper,' Dusty told her. 'We'd brought in a herd of beef he needed to feed the Tejas.'

'They need feeding,' Ma commented, watching the men sit at the table.

'I was right pleased when Lon told me you were on the stage, Jeanie,' Dusty remarked. 'Figured you could take us to Ma. It got better when I found out you're staying in town. We need fifty horses for the OD Connected and Double B remudas. Can you get them for us, Ma?'

'I reckon so. How soon do you want them?'

'As quick as you can,' Dusty told her. 'Spreads're going to need more horses if this idea of Uncle Charlie Goodnight's comes off.'

'What idea's that?' Jeanie asked, for Colonel Charles Goodnight stood at the peak of the cattle industry.

'Him and Oliver Loving's been driving cattle to Fort Sumner, over to New Mexico,' Dusty explained. 'Well, he figures to take three thousand head later this year——'

'*Three* thousand!' Jeanie gasped.

'The Army'll buy them to feed the Apaches on the reservations,' Mark told her. 'But that's only part of it.'

'Sure,' Dusty agreed. 'If that many can be handled, we figure to try driving them to the railroad in Kansas.'

'If it can be done, it'll be the answer to where we can sell our beef,' Mark went on soberly. 'Sure it'll be hard, but a herd that size'll pay for the taking.'

'Handling the herd's going to call for four to six horses a man,' Dusty said. 'So we'll need more of them.'

'We'll get them for you,' Ma promised. 'The Kid allows he's working for you, Dusty.'

'He is,' the small Texan grinned. 'He met up with us at the post. Was coming here, but he saw Arnie Hogan riding out of town with a Mexican and figured to look around. Where's Kenny at?'

'He went to the hotel,' Ma replied. 'I allowed he'd best go side that Scotch feller who was on the stage if the Flores boys come calling.'

'We saw that feller's name on the register at the hotel when we went for rooms,' Mark said, 'Happen he's kin to Major Angus Farquharson who ran my company in Sheldon's Cavalry, I'd say he can look after himself.'

In the Black Bear Saloon, Colin Farquharson looked like he was to be given a chance to prove Mark's words.

Every instinct Colin possessed warned him of danger. He felt sure that the incident had gone farther than a quarrel following a senseless, tasteless and unfunny piece of horseplay. A sideways glance at Kenny's set, grim face, taken with the menacing behaviour of the four men facing them and the attitude of the watching crowd confirmed his suspicions. Angus Farquharson had often mentioned the quick tempers of the Texans and commented on their way of settling arguments with roaring guns.

'Let's go, Colin,' Kenny said quietly after delivering his warning.

For all the even manner in which he spoke, Kenny knew the danger. While competent with his Colt, he lacked the flashing, deadly speed of a top gun fighter. Maybe he stood a chance of taking one of the four with him, but he was sure to be killed. Guessing what Branch had in mind, Kenny knew that backing down offered no answer. Branch's bunch would continue to goad Colin until the Scot resisted. When that happened, Kenny would again be drawn into conflict. So Kenny figured that the affair had best be settled straight away.

'You know how it is, Kenny boy,' Branch said mockingly. 'If we let him go without showing us now, we'd be laughed out of town. So we can't let him go.'

A double clicking sound reached Branch's ears. While not as famous as it would become, he recognised it as the noise made by a Henry rifle's loading mechanism at work. Branch and his companions looked into the bar mirror and discovered that another player sat in the game. Or stood in on it. A tall, slim, baby-faced youngster, dressed all in black, propped open the batwing doors, handling a short repeating rifle with casual competence.

'You want to bet you can't?' asked the Ysabel Kid.

With that, he strolled across the room. He carried the Winchester in his right hand, with his forefinger inside the triggerguard and the other three curled through the lever, the barrel resting on his right shoulder.

Watching the Kid come towards him, Colin was reminded of a caged leopard he had once seen. There was the same latent, controlled deadly ease of movement, the warning that he could explode into blindingly fast movement. From the Kid, Colin turned his eyes to his tormentors. All but Branch showed uneasiness as the black-dressed youngster came to a halt at Colin's left side.

'Who asked you to bill in?' Branch demanded belligerently.

'Easy, Spring!' Moore whispered urgently. 'That's the Ysabel Kid.'

Instantly a change came over Branch. While he had not recognised the Kid, he was fully aware of the other's reputation. Stacking up against Kenny Schell and the unarmed Scot suddenly lost all its attraction, when to do so also meant taking on the Ysabel Kid. So a weak grin twisted at his lips.

'Hell, we were only kidding,' Branch declared. 'The boys just wanted to know what the feller wears under his skirt.'

'He killed Adán Flores for trying to find out,' the Kid replied. 'So if you bunch've a mind to see, come ahead.'

Having flung down his challenge, the Kid stood in relaxed readiness to meet any attempt to take it up. So did Kenny, his hand hovering to scoop the Army Colt from its holster at the first hostile move.

None came. Instead Branch shrugged and said, 'We'll forget it if he feels that strong about it. Come on, boys. Let's go drink someplace where they ain't so all-fired touchy.'

'Mister,' the Kid put in, stopping Branch in mid-turn. 'Should anything happen to these two gents, accidental-like, I'll come looking for you—and I fight real dirty.'

'We'll mind it,' Branch promised and stamped from the saloon followed by his men. None of them offered to as much as look back, for fear that the Kid might regard doing so as a hostile act.

On the street, the Trimbles and Moore took turns in describing the Kid's ancestry and possible fate using the most lurid terms they could lay tongue to. All the time, however, they walked at a fair clip away from the Black Bear Saloon.

'What're we going to do now, Sprig?' Moore inquired.

'What can we do?' Branch replied. 'You boys want to lay for 'em as they come out?'

'Naw!' Eric Trimble stated emphatically.

'Folks might call it murder,' Sam went on. 'We could get Kenny on his lonesome——'

'You figure the Kid didn't mean what he said?' Moore inquired derisively. 'If you do, lay for Kenny. But don't ask me to go along.'

'Huh!' Branch snorted. 'What're we worrying over? The Army'll not be so eager to give them the contract with Trader dead.'

With which consolation, he led the way into another saloon.

After the quartet had left, Kenny gave a long sigh and turned towards the bar. 'Let's have three drinks, bar-keep,' he said. 'Kid, you were as welcome as rain in a dry summer.'

'Likely,' the Kid answered dryly and looked at Colin. 'Friend, if you're going to keep on wearing that kilt, you'd best start to pack a gun.'

Chapter Six

Carefully Colin Farquharson poured a measure of powder into the left-hand barrel of the pistol he held. Its mate lay in the open box on the bed at his side, along with the cased pair's accessories. Working with smooth precision, he rammed the charge and its wad down the barrel then followed it with the rest of the load. He had already attended to the other barrel, so he fitted the percussion caps in place and set the hammers at half-cock. For a moment he sat looking at the second pistol, then decided not to bother with it.

Hearing a knock on the door, he crossed the room and opened it.

'Howdy,' greeted Kenny Schell, entering. 'Ma says for you to come over and have breakfast with us.'

'That's kind of her,' Colin said, and meant it. 'How did you know where to find me?'

'Met the Kid going out,' Kenny explained. 'He told me that he'd changed rooms with you last night.'

'So he did, although I'd never have thought a man like him would be superstitious.'

With the departure of Branch and his men from the Black Bear, Colin had spent a pleasant evening at the saloon. April Hosman joined them, then later Dusty Fog, Mark Counter and a couple of the OD Connected cowhands arrived. There had been four Scots among the soldiers, all highly delighted to see their native dress again. Nor did their delight lessen when Colin admitted to having a set of bagpipes in his baggage. Encouraged by the Scottish soldiers and his companions, he had collected the bagpipes and entertained the customers of the saloon to a selection of Highland tunes.

On their return to the hotel, the Kid had asked Colin to change rooms with him explaining that seven was a bad luck number for the Comanche, whereas room twelve, which Colin rented, was guaranteed to give a member of the *Pehnane* good fortune. Although slightly amused at such primitive superstition, Colin had agreed to the exchange. He did not realise that the Kid had really made the request in case of a visit by the Flores brothers.

'Where're Dusty, Mark and the Kid?' Colin inquired as he buckled on his belt.

'Over to the livery barn, tending to their hosses,' Kenny replied and indicated the pistol case. 'That's a right fancy pair of hand-guns you've got. Don't you have a revolver?'

'No.'

'It'll likely be best for you to stick with the kind of guns you know,' Kenny admitted. 'Let's go. Ma's waiting breakfast for us and don't take to being kept from her victuals in the morning.'

The weather being mild, Colin dispensed with jacket, vest and plaid. Appearing in one's shirt appeared to be socially acceptable, so he went along with the local custom. After sliding the pistol in the loop on the left side of his belt, with the dirk still in place at the right, he put on his bonnet.

Grinning, Kenny watched Colin set the hat at its usual jaunty angle. On first being told to go and guard the Scot, he had felt a touch resentful, figuring a feller who wore a skirt could not be masculine. From the first meeting, though, he had revised his opinion. While he figured that Colin needed educating in some matters, he now regarded the Scot as a man to ride the river with.

On leaving the hotel, Colin received his first daylight view of Fort Sawyer. It was not an impressive sight. The town's main business premises, stores, saloons and such, shared the main street with the

Overland Stage line's depot and the building which housed the local law. Behind the street lay the homes of the citizens, scattered without any worry about civic planning. Although the front of the livery barn opened on to the street, its corral was at the rear.

'We'll go collect Dusty, Mark and the Kid,' Kenny remarked as he and Colin stood on the sidewalk. 'The corral's on the way to our house.'

'Lead on,' Colin answered, looking along the street. 'The Black Bear opens early.'

Following the direction of the Scot's gaze, Kenny nodded. A horse stood tethered in front of the saloon and its main doors were open.

'Harve Jute's the owner,' Kenny commented. 'He don't take to missing the chance of trade. Has the place opened soon after sun-up. A feller can go in, buy a drink and watch the gals eating breakfast has a mind to.' He grinned. 'We'll go there if you like.'

'Not if your mother is waiting breakfast, for us,' Colin decided.

'I do admire a man with good sense,' Kenny chuckled. 'Come on, afore that lil sister of mine eats everything off the table.'

'That's a fine-looking horse,' Colin remarked as they walked across the street in the direction of the livery barn, indicating an animal hitched to the rail before the end of a general store next to the barn.

'The *bayo naranjado*?' Kenny replied. 'It's not bad. I like mine a touch less flashy.'

As he spoke, Kenny's eyes automatically took in certain details about the horse. First he noticed the single-girthed saddle with a horn the size of a dinner-plate. No Texan normally rode such a rig; and few Mexican vaqueros owned such an expensive outfit. Then Kenny became aware that the reins hung over the hitching rail instead of being tied around it. Putting the two facts together, Kenny drew a conclusion which rang out a warning for him—an instant too late.

Standing in the alley, looking along the street, Vicente Flores sucked in a breath of excitement. The man who had killed his brother Adán left the hotel and came in his direction. There could be no doubt about it. No other man in Fort Sawyer wore such outlandish clothes. It seemed that the wounded Arturo and later Arnaldo Hogan had spoke the truth about the man's appearance. He really did wear a skirt.

With cold, calculating eyes, Vicente studied his intended victim. It was a pity that the man in the skirt was walking with a companion, but not too great an obstacle. Neither of them appeared to suspect his presence and would be unprepared when he made his appearance. While the Texan wore a Colt, he did not have the undefinable air of being fast with it. As for the man who killed Adán, he had nothing better than an old-fashioned, muzzle-loading pistol thrust into his belt. Vicente nodded with satisfaction. A quick step from behind concealment, two shots fired and he would be on his horse, heading out of town, leaving Adán's killer dead or dying on the ground. Then Vicente would see what Tiburcio and Matteo had to say. He, Vicente, the youngest member of the family, would have avenged their dead brother while the other two waited outside town in the hope that the man in the skirt would come to them.

Instead of taking the bodies to the mission as Tiburcio ordered, Vicente and Manuel had left the rest of the party in the dark. Thirsting for revenge on the woman who had killed his brother, Manuel went willingly along with Vicente's scheme. They had stayed well clear of Onion Creek and arrived on the outskirts of Fort Sawyer shortly after midnight. Waiting at Arnaldo Hogan's house until he returned, they had learned all he knew. More than that, he had explained how Tiburcio planned to wait until Adán's killer left town before striking. Hogan was to watch and report to Tiburcio when the man boarded a stagecoach to continue his journey.

Such a plan had small appeal to Vicente. The camp on Onion Creek offered none of the luxuries he craved. Especially as Hogan could not say when the man might be leaving. So he had decided on his course of action. Putting aside any notion of finding the man at the hotel, he had waited until morning. Then, while Manuel went to the Black Bear Saloon in search of the woman, Vicente had left his horse loose-hitched close by ready for a fast departure and waited in hiding for the man to appear.

Cold pleasure filled Vicente as he drew and cocked his right-hand Colt. For years Tiburcio and Matteo had regarded him as a stupid, head-strong boy; handy for doing casual killing but not worth including in their planning sessions. After this morning's work, that would all be changed. While the older brothers waited outside town, Vicente had ridden in and avenged the family honour.

Better not let them come too close, Vicente decided. That Texan might prove better with his gun than appeared on the surface. No, it would be safer to step out while they were still some thirty yards away. At that distance, there was less chance of being hit at the end of a fast draw.

With that thought in mind, Vicente gripped the Navy Colt in both hands. He sprang out of the alley, raising the gun shoulder high and taking sight on the man who had killed his brother.

'Look out!' Kenny yelled, throwing himself sideways to crash into Colin.

Moving as he did, Kenny saved Colin and placed himself in danger. The force of the impact knocked Colin staggering, but its impetus carried Kenny into the place where the Scot had stood. Before Vicente could correct his aim, the Colt's hammer fell. The bullet meant for Colin ripped into Kenny's chest. Giving a croaking cry, he started to fall. Muttering an annoyed curse, Vicente cocked the Colt on the recoil and brought its barrel around in Colin's direction. A faint grin twisted at Vicente's lips as he watched the Scot start to slide the pistol free. There would be little enough danger from it in the hands of a man who wore women's clothes. Without haste, Vicente began to take his aim, little knowing he was making the biggest mistake of his life.

In Scotland, Colin's family had for generations held the post of *an gillecoise*, the henchman, senior bodyguard to the chief of the clan. In attendance to the chief at all times, the henchman stood fully armed behind his leader's chair at banquets. One of the required qualities for the post had been the ability to draw and fire a pistol with some speed. Although that particular skill was no longer needed, tradition demanded that the henchman possessed it. So Colin and his older brothers had received instruction in using the pistol along with lessons on handling the claymore and dirk.

Curling his fingers about the pistol's butt, Colin started to slip it free from the belt-loop. Working in concert, his left hand drew back the twin hammers. By the time he came to a halt from Kenny's shove, Colin held a fully cocked weapon in his right hand. Instinctively he saw that there would be no time to duplicate the Mexican's method of shooting, but knew it did not matter.

With the pistol still at waist level, Colin squeezed the right-side barrel's trigger. Giving a deep crack, the weapon discharged its load. Not a solid ball, but a cloud of Number 12 shot pellets. On the heels of the first shot, Colin cut loose from the second barrel.

The first hail of pellets arrived just as Vicente began to squeeze his Colt's trigger. Tearing into his body, they jerked him on to his heels and caused him to flinch. Not much, but enough. Colin heard the bullet split the air by his ear. Then the second charge of shot struck the *bandido*, peppering his throat and face with red spots. Again Vicente jolted on his heels. Turning slowly around, he dropped the revolver, collided with the wall of the nearest building, bounced from it to the ground. Snorting, the *bayo naranjado* pulled free its reins and began to run along the street away from the sound of the shooting.

Shock numbed Colin for a moment as he realised that he had once again been forced to shoot a man. People going about their business on the street turned and made for the young Scot. Others appeared from various buildings. A low groan drew Colin's attention to Kenny and caused him to forget his own feelings. Clutching at his right side, the young mustanger tried to rise. Colin let the pistol fall and was dropping to his knees at Kenny's side when he saw Dusty Fog, Mark Counter and the Ysabel Kid come through the doors of the livery barn. Bounding forward, the Kid grabbed the *bayo naranjado's* reins and brought it to a halt. Then he followed his companions towards Colin.

'That's Vicente Flores!' the Kid ejaculated, looking down. 'Likely the rest of 'em're here, Dusty.'

After leaving Colin the previous night, the Kid had commented on the likelihood of the Flores gang coming into Fort Sawyer to take revenge on the man who killed Adán. Being aware of how Tiburcio and Matteo regarded Vicente, the Kid felt it highly unlikely that they would send in their younger brother to handle the task alone. That meant there was danger for everybody who had been on the stagecoach. The Flores boys would hardly be satisfied with just killing the young Scot.

Appreciating the latter point, Dusty snapped his orders. 'Head for Ma's place, Lon. See to Kenny, Mark.'

Even while speaking, Dusty's eyes searched the surrounding area for signs of the rest of the gang. One of the things a Comanche learned early was that a horse could move a whole heap faster than any man on foot. So the Kid caught hold of the horn and vaulted afork the *bayo naranjado's* fancy saddle. Clamping hold with his knees, he fetched the horse around in a tight turn and set it moving through the alley as the quickest way to reach the Schell's temporary home.

'Get the doctor here!' Mark barked at the approaching people and one turned to obey.

Dusty's scrutiny had covered the buildings as far as the Black Bear Saloon without locating any more members of the Flores gang. A number of people came from the saloon, girls wearing long robes and no make-up and male employees in their shirt sleeves. Clearly they had only emerged to discover the cause of the shooting, not in flight or as cover for *bandidos*. On the verge of ignoring them, Dusty saw the horse standing at the hitching rail. Even from where he stood, Dusty could tell that it carried a Mexican saddle.

A Mexican's horse being outside the saloon, even at that early hour, might be no more than coincidence. Dusty could not take a chance on it. April Hosman, another of the stagecoach's passengers and an active participant in busting up the robbery worked there.

'Watch things, Mark!' Dusty ordered and started to run along the street.

Approaching the end of the building, Dusty heard the crack of a shot from inside. The employees on the sidewalk turned, milling around, chattering and looking over the batwing doors but none of them offered to enter.

Standing at the bar, Manuel waited for the appearance of the woman who had killed his brother. A protesting Arnaldo Hogan had been compelled to accompany Manuel to the saloon. Looking through a window, Hogan had stated that all the girls, except the newcomer, were at breakfast. However Hogan had insisted that the blonde woman lived in the saloon, having heard one of the girls comment on the matter previous to her arrival. So Manuel had allowed Hogan to scuttle away. Leaving his horse loose-hitched to the rail, the *bandido* had entered the building. He saw the *bayo naranjado* along the street, but ignored it. What Vicente Flores did was his own concern. Manuel cared only about avenging Jaime.

Nobody had shown surprise when the *bandido* entered. After serving him, the bartender rejoined the men and girls sitting taking a leisurely breakfast. Then shots cracked along the street, drawing the attention of the room's occupants to the outside. Pushing back their chairs, the men and women made for the front doors but Manuel did not follow them. He cared little for the cause of the shooting. Maybe Vicente had met the man who dressed in a skirt. Manuel felt disinterested in the outcome. With the blonde woman dead, he intended to return to Mexico and join another *bandido* gang.

Hearing footsteps on the balcony, Manuel looked up. He saw a tall, shapely woman wearing a flimsy robe over a nightgown at the head of the stairs; a blonde, good-looking in the gringo fashion. Quickly Manuel studied the situation. Not far from the stairs, a door opened on to a side alley. After shooting the woman, he could go out that way. Then, when the other saloon workers entered, a quick dash along the sidewalk would take him to his horse.

With his plans made, he slipped his Colt from its holster and turned. On the point of asking Manuel what the shooting was about, April saw him swing towards her. The expression of savage hate brought her to a halt, then she saw the revolver in his hand.

'Wha——!' April began, still unable to believe that the man planned to shoot.

Flame sparked from the Colt and the bullet ploughed a furrow in the bannister rail at her side. Taking an involuntary step to the rear, April tripped and sat down. With horrified eyes, she watched the Mexican re-cock his revolver and start moving towards her. At that moment she recalled that her Remington Double Derringer was in the drawer of her room's dressing-table. Going to breakfast in the bar room had not seemed to call for weapons. She bitterly regretted the decision as she watched Manuel's slow advance. Throwing a glance at the batwing doors, she saw her fellow-workers looking over them but not coming in. That figured. None of them were armed either.

Looking at the crowd hovering before the saloon's front entrance, Dusty gave up any idea of using it. Swiftly he thought over what he remembered about the lay-out of the building. There was a side door along the alley he was approaching. Entering that way would be quicker and more unexpected than trying to charge through the men and women on the sidewalk.

With Dusty, to think was to act. However he always thought first. Swerving around the corner, he sprinted down the alley. So far he had not drawn his Colts and decided against doing it until after he knew whether the door was locked. Trying it would be inviting trouble, so Dusty took the more obvious step of assuming the key had been turned.

Dropping his left shoulder, he gathered himself for the effort. Then he charged forward, throwing every ounce of weight and atom of strength in his small, powerful body at the door. He struck the wood, feeling it yielding under the impact. For a moment he thought that the door would hold. With a click, the lock snapped apart and the door swung inwards. Carried by his impetus, Dusty plunged into the barroom.

Lining his gun at April, Manuel stalked closer. He guessed that he had little time to kill the woman and make good his escape, so he did not intend to miss. Just as he prepared to squeeze the trigger, he heard a crash and the side door burst open. Taking his eyes to the source of the noise, the *bandido* saw Dusty Fog enter. Only it was not the small, insignificant cowhand one usually saw. Somehow Dusty seemed to have taken on size and heft, becoming a *big*, dangerous man.

Across flashed Dusty's right hand, closing on the bone handle of the left-side Colt. All in one incredibly swift move, he slid the weapon from its holster, cocked it, placed his finger on the trigger and touched off a shot. Three-quarters of a second after the hand's first movement, a bullet spun through the seven-and-a-half inch barrel of the Army Colt and punctured a hole between Manuel's eyes.

Dusty shot fast, without hesitation, for an instant kill. There could be no reasoning with a vengeance-crazed Mexican *bandido* and any delay might have proved fatal for the woman on the stairs. For all Dusty's speed, there was little margin to spare.

Even as the bullet shattered into his brain, Manuel got off another shot. If Dusty had delayed, it would have buried itself into April's body. However the .44 ball made the *bandido* stagger at the moment when the hammer began to fall. Splinters flew from the stairs less than an inch to her left. Then Manuel's fingers opened and he crumpled to the floor.

Slowly April drew herself erect. Sucking in a deep breath, she tore her eyes from Manuel and turned them in Dusty's direction.

'Why'd he want to kill me?' she asked.

'He's one of the Flores gang,' the small Texan explained. 'You'd best come with me, ma'am.'

'Where to?' she gulped, glancing to where the other employees were coming through the front doors.

'Jeanie Schell's house,' Dusty replied. 'If the rest of the gang's around, I reckon you'll be safer there.'

'Bu—But I'm not dressed!' April squealed, indicating the nightgown under her robe.

'This's no time to worry about female vanity, ma'am!' Dusty growled. 'Let's go.'

Chapter Seven

Following April Hosman into the front room of the Schell house, Dusty found Mark and Colin already there. The young Scot slumped in a chair at the table, his head resting on his hands. Despite the urgency of the situation, April had insisted on dressing before she accompanied Dusty. Knowing how 'good' women usually regarded saloon-workers, she figured being accepted by Ma Schell would prove hard enough without rolling up in her revealing night-clothes.

'Where's Lon, Mark?' Dusty asked.

'He went down to the stage depot to warn Lou Temple,' the blond giant answered. 'We got Kenny back here. The doctor's with him now.'

'He pushed me aside,' Colin put in, his voice hoarse. 'If he hadn't, he would still be all right.'

'Take it easy, Colin,' Dusty said gently. 'I don't reckon anybody blames you for what happened.'

'But it w——'

A knock on the door caused Colin to chop off his words. At another time he might have been interested in, or marvelled at, the speed with which Mark and Dusty each drew a revolver. Slowly the Scot turned his eyes towards the door, watching the cautious manner in which Dusty went towards it.

'Who is it?' the small Texan called.

'Sheriff Lansing.'

Still holding his Colt in the left hand, Dusty drew open the door. Strain showed on Lansing's fat face as he looked around the room. Holstering his Colt, Dusty closed the door.

'How's Kenny?' Lansing inquired.

'The doctor's working on him,' Mark answered, dropping his revolver into leather.

'It's the Flores gang, ain't it?' the sheriff went on.

'Sure,' Dusty agreed. 'They tried for Colin and Miss Hosman here. Colin dropped one of 'em and I downed the other.'

Which, as Lansing knew, still left fifteen or more of the gang to be accounted for. Sucking in a nervous breath, he glanced at April then studied the two Texans' air of alert readiness.

'Reckon the rest of 'em're in town, Cap'n Fog?'

'Could be, sheriff. I don't see Tiburcio sending in just two men. Happen you're going to make the rounds, Mark, the Kid and I'll come with you.'

Such a thought had not entered the sheriff's head. In fact he had considered only the possible danger to himself when hearing who was involved in the shooting. Before Lansing could decide on an answer, one of the bedroom doors opened and Ma came out. Her eyes went first to April, then to Dusty.

'How is it, Ma?' Dusty asked.

'He'll live, but he'll not be riding for a fair spell.'

'Flores' bunch're after Miss Hosman as well as Colin,' the small Texan explained as Ma again looked at the blonde. 'One of them tried to kill her at the Black Bear, I figured she'd be safer here.'

'You could be right,' Ma admitted. 'Make yourself to home, girlie. It's likely not what you're used to, but it'll beat getting killed.'

'Reckon you can tend to things here, Ma?' Dusty asked.

'I reckon I can. Why?'

'Could be the rest of the gang're around town. Sheriff here'll need company when he goes to take a look.'

Knowing Lansing, Ma figured that the suggestion to search the town had not originated from him. However she wasted no time in debating the matter.

Backed by Dusty Fog, the Ysabel Kid and that big, handsome Mark Counter, the sheriff should be able to chase the Flores gang out of town. So she nodded her agreement.

'It'll be best. Can you handle a gun, girlie?'

'You load it, put it in my hands, set a *bandido* up not too far in front of it and I'll give it a whirl. And the name's "April", "Girlie's" the fat red head.'

A grin twisted at Ma's lips. 'I allus wondered about that. Make yourself to home while I get the scatter from my bedroom.'

'Mrs. Schell,' Colin put in, lifting his head and turned a worried face to Ma. 'I—I don't know what to say to you. It was all my fault. Kenny pushed me aside and——'

'He allus was one for acting reckless,' Ma replied, walking to the Scot's side and laying a hand on his shoulder. 'Now don't go fretting boy. None of us blame you for what happened. Back on the stage, they'd've killed all of you happen you hadn't give the Kid a chance to start fighting. And today Vicente Flores wouldn't've stopped just by shooting you, he'd've killed Kenny and anybody else who got in his way.'

'Ma's right on that,' Mark put in, checking his Colts. 'Are you set to go, sheriff?'

'Do you have a gun I can borrow, Mrs. Schell?' Colin asked before Lansing answered the question. 'I want to go with Dusty and Mark.'

'Take that one,' Ma replied, waving a hand in the direction of the fireplace and crossing to enter her bedroom.

Rising, Colin walked over to the fireplace. Although Ma had meant for him to take the Sharps carbine, Colin misunderstood her. Instead, he lifted the ivory-handled Dragoon Colt from the wall. After shooting Vicente, Colin had suddenly realised that he held an empty pistol, a weapon which required considerable time to reload. So he felt that, if he must be involved in further fighting, he needed a firearm carrying more than two shots. The big Dragoon Colt was not unknown to him. Its maker, Colonel Sam Colt, was a salesman of note and did not overlook the British Isles as a market for his products. Several of Colin's uncles were army officers and had bought the big revolvers to carry as a side-arm. The young Scot had done enough shooting with one to figure he could handle the Dragoon from above the fireplace.

Just as Colin took down the gun, Jeanie walked from Kenny's bedroom where she had been helping the doctor. Letting out an indignant yell, she stamped across in Colin's direction.

'What in hell're you doing?' she hissed.

'Ma said Colin could take a gun, Jeanie,' Dusty said, for Colin just stood and stared at the girl's furious face.

'Not *that* gun!' Jeanie hissed.

'I thought it would be a better weapon——' Colin began.

'What do you know about weapons?' Jeanie interrupted hotly. 'That was my pappy's gun. He was a forty-four caliber man. He never needed anybody to——'

'That's enough!'

Having heard Jeanie's comments from the bedroom, Ma burst into her daughter's presence and snapped out a command that halted further comment. The last thing Ma wanted was to increase Colin's concern at causing Kenny to be wounded. If Jeanie finished her words, Colin would know why Kenny happened to be along with him. Ma could imagine how the young Scot would feel then.

To be fair to her, Jeanie was not acting out of spite or petty meanness. Still smarting under the memory of her Uncle Jabez's behaviour, she was extra touchy about her father's memory and property. That, combined with worry and anger at Kenny's injury brought on her outburst. She was already regretting her words when Ma appeared, but the intervention only gave the girl's contrary streak an added stiffness.

'He's no right to use pappy's gun!' Jeanie insisted.

'I've never slapped you down in front of folks,' Ma growled, face burning red with annoyance. 'But, happen you don't shut up, I'll make a start.'

'Mrs. Schell,' Colin said. 'I'll use the carbine.'

'You can take the Colt if you want it,' Ma replied, and although she stiffened slightly, Jeanie did not speak.

'The wee rifle'll be good enough, ma'am,' Colin assured her. 'If you'll be so good as to let me have bullets for it.'

'It's capped ready,' Ma said. 'I'll get you a box of cartridges.'

While her mother returned to the bedroom, Jeanie stood glaring at Colin. Fully aware that Ma did not make idle threats, and more than a little ashamed at her own behaviour, the girl knew better than to continue her attack. Realising that she was in the wrong did little to make Jeanie feel more amiable to Colin. Instead she regarded his silence and Ma's intervention as further proof of his lack of masculinity. It seemed that somebody else was always having to finish the trouble he had started.

Taking the box of paper cartridges Ma brought from the bedroom, Colin thanked her and turned to Jeanie.

'I'm sorry, M——'

Letting out an indignant snort, the girl tossed her head. She turned and went into Kenny's bedroom, started to slam the door, realised what she was doing and grabbed at the handle. Completing the closing in silence, she gave an annoyed hiss. That fancy-dressed dude had the damnedest way of putting a burr under her saddle.

'Come on, *amigo*,' Dusty said gently to Colin and then looked at Lansing. 'We're ready, sheriff. Where do we start?'

Which put Lansing in an awkward position. Appointed by the Davis Administration, he held his post on political rather than efficiency grounds. Faced with a serious situation, he had no idea how to deal with it. Up until the question, he had assumed that

Dusty Fog would take command and was content to go along in a subordinate capacity.

'I—We'll go through the greaser section,' the sheriff decided after a brief pause to marshal his thoughts. 'I reckon the Flores bunch'd be hid out with their own kind.'

'Could be,' Dusty admitted and opened the door. 'Will you be all right, Ma?'

'If we ain't, we'll let you know,' Ma promised.

'Especially if I get that scatter-gun I was promised,' April remarked.

'I'll fetch it now,' Ma grunted. 'All this talking's made me forget it.'

As the men went on to the porch; they found the Kid and Temple approaching. Each of the men looked well armed. In addition to their belt guns, they both carried two rifles. The Kid had his Winchester in his right hand and a shorter version of it in the left, while Temple toted a Spencer carbine and another of the new model Winchesters.

'Figured we might need these,' the Kid commented, hefting the two Winchesters. 'So I fetched 'em from the hotel.'

'Made me tote the heavy 'n',' Temple went on, holding out the Winchester. 'Here, take hold of it, Mark.'

'Sheriff figures we should go through the Mex section, Lon,' Dusty remarked as he accepted his carbine.

'I've already done that,' the Kid answered. 'They not hid down there.'

'You searched every *jacale* and the cantina?' Lansing asked.

'Warn't no need,' the Kid replied. 'Folks weren't acting scared or nothing. They would've been if the Flores boys were around.'

'Maybe we should make a search,' Lansing said to Dusty. 'You know greasers?'

'Nowhere near as well as Lon does,' Dusty stated. 'I'll go along with him.'

'There's one way we can maybe fetch 'em out of

wherever they're hid,' Mark put in. 'If Colin's game to try it.'

'Try what?' the Scot asked.

'Walk right down the centre of main street. If they're around, that ought to bring them out.'

'It for sure will,' the Kid agreed. 'They'll have to make their play, or lose face with the local Mexicans.'

'I'll do it!' Colin said grimly.

'It'll be risky,' Dusty warned. 'You'll be throwing out a challenge they have to take up.'

'I'll still do it!' Colin insisted.

'Figured you would,' Dusty grinned. 'Well do everything we can to make things easier.'

'Give Lon and me a few minutes to get into place, Dusty,' Mark suggested. 'I'll go to the livery barn.'

'Saloon for me,' the Kid went on. 'Up on the balcony.'

'Take my carbine with you, Lon,' Dusty ordered. 'You'd best stay here with Ma, Lou. How about you, sheriff?'

'M—Me?' Lansing croaked.

'Maybe you'd best go back to your office and get your deputies ready to help us when Flores comes,' Dusty suggested.

'Yeah!' Lansing agreed eagerly. 'That's what I'll do.'

'Shouldn't he be with us?' Colin inquired, watching the sheriff scuttle away.

'Comes to trouble,' Dusty replied dryly, 'I'd sooner have him where he is, out from under-foot. Get to it, Mark, Lon. We'll come on to the street down the west end.'

After Mark and the Kid took their departure, the latter once more carrying Dusty's carbine, the small Texan turned his attention to Colin. Making sure the Scot knew how to load and handle the Sharps, Dusty told him what to do in case of an attack. From all he could see and the questions Colin asked, Dusty concluded his instructions had been understood and he could rely on the other not to panic. While walking towards the west side of the town, Colin brought up something which had been puzzling him since hearing Jeanie mention it.

'What does it mean when you say somebody is a forty-four caliber man?'

'It started back around the early '40s,' Dusty explained. 'Colonel Colt's new revolvers started coming into Texas about then. His first guns were only .36 caliber, and the new gun was a forty-four. Which same was a whole heap of gun, too much for some folks. The Texas Rangers got the first of the new guns, and the Rangers were all picked men. So folks started saying they were forty-four caliber men, something special. As time went on, more of the Colts came on the market. The name got to mean a feller who was all man and could be relied on from hell to high water. Any man who gets called it earns the name.'

'Miss Schell's father was a forty-four caliber man?'

'All the way and back again.'

By that time they had passed alongside the last building and stood at the edge of the main street. Carefully Dusty studied the surrounding range, then turned his eyes to the street. The body had been removed and only a few people walked the street.

'Let's go,' Dusty said. 'Take it easy and keep your eyes open.'

Knowing that Mark and the Kid were covering them did not cause Dusty to relax or become careless. All the time he and Colin walked, he kept his eyes constantly flickering from side to side. On the sidewalks, men and women paused to look at them as they advanced along the centre of the street. No westerner needed to ask what such behaviour meant and there was a sudden scattering as the people headed for cover.

As they passed the livery barn, Colin saw Mark standing up in the hay-loft. The blond giant gave the Scot a cheery grin, but did not speak or lower his rifle. Walking from the barn towards the Black Bear

Saloon, Colin tried to locate the Kid. At first he failed, then saw the black-dressed youngster crouching behind the long name-board fastened to the railings of the balcony.

Suddenly hooves drummed on the street behind them and four riders tore into view from around the end of a building. Instantly the Kid rose from his place of concealment. His left hand tossed the carbine down to Dusty and his right started to raise the rifle shoulder-wards. Catching the carbine, Dusty swivelled around. Colin turned almost as fast, snapping the Sharps to his shoulder.

'Don't shoot!' Mark bellowed, appearing at the loft's loading door. The riders wore U.S. cavalry uniforms and forage caps. Nor was it likely that were members of the Flores gang in disguise, for all had Anglo-Saxon features. Finding two carbines on the street aimed their way, the soldiers reined in their horses hurriedly.

'What the——!' the sergeant in the lead began.

'We thought you were somebody else,' Colin replied, lowering his Sharps.

'Looks that way,' the non-com admitted dryly, then studied the Scot from head to toe. 'Say! You're the feller who shot Adán Flores, ain't you?'

'He's the feller,' Dusty agreed. 'We figured Adán's kin might be wanting to try for evens and concluded to give them a chance.'

'So that's why you're out here,' the sergeant breathed.

'Figured letting them come to us'd be the easiest way to find them,' Dusty explained. 'And when you boys come busting around the corner——'

'Yeah,' the non-com said. 'We was headed for the saloon to spend some of our pay afore the post sutler attaches it. If we'd got shot, it'd've riled him. We owe him a double-eagle a piece.'

'I've got me a thirst worse than afore,' commented one of the soldiers.

'And me,' admitted the sergeant. 'We'll go on, if that's all right with you, si—friend.'

'Go to it,' Dusty told him. 'I hope you spend some afore the sutler finds out you've left the post.'

'We'll try,' promised the sergeant. 'If there's any shooting, we'll come out and lend a hand.'

'Thanks,' Dusty said.

After the soldiers had ridden on, the Kid walked from the saloon. Mark came from the livery barn and joined his companions.

'What do you reckon?' Dusty asked.

'They're not around,' Mark replied. 'Or if they are, the soldiers'll keep them off.'

'Way I see it,' the Kid went on. 'Vicente and the other jasper came in without Tiburcio knowing.'

'He felt that bad about Adán being killed?' Dusty inquired.

'Felt nothing,' scoffed the Kid. 'He'd do it to show Tiburcio and Matteo how tough he was. Other feller was maybe kin to the jasper Miss April shot.'

'So the gang may not be here after all?' Colin said.

'They're around, somewheres not too far off,' the Kid stated. 'Arnie Ho—— Hell's fire, Dusty. I clean forgot to look in on ole Arnie while I was down there.'

'Do it now,' Dusty ordered. 'Do you want Mark along?'

'I can handle it best alone,' the Kid decided.

'We'll wait for you at Ma Schell's then,' Dusty replied.

'Where can I buy a revolver?' Colin asked as the Kid strolled unconcernedly off in the direction of the Mexican quarter.

'Down to Hoffer's store,' Dusty answered. 'I'll come with you. Mark, you'd best go back to let Ma know what's happened.'

'Sure,' Mark agreed. 'Only don't come blaming Lon and me if the Flores bunch sneak up and kill you both.'

With that friendly warning ringing in their ears, Dusty and Colin headed for Hoffer's general store. A few customers eyed them worriedly as they entered, but said nothing about the incident in the street. The store carried the usual miscellany of items, including a good range of firearms. Crossing to the side of the shop devoted to sporting goods, Dusty and Colin looked into the glass-topped case which held a number of revolvers.

'I'd like to look at that one,' Colin said, pointing to the required gun as Hoffer joined them.

Tall, lean, with an expression of concern permanently on his face, Hoffer studied the choice for a moment. 'Sure. I've got some new 1860 Army Colts if——'

'That's the one I want,' Colin insisted, still indicating the old Dragoon model.

'Mind if I look it over?' Dusty asked.

'Feel free, Cap'n Fog,' Hoffer replied, opening the case and taking out the revolver. 'I got it from the widow of an old Ranger. It's been well cared for.'

Accepting and examining the Dragoon, Dusty saw that Hoffer had spoken the truth about its condition. However he wondered if the lighter Army Colt might be more suitable for the young Scot.

'No!' Colin stated vehemently when Dusty raised the point. 'This's the kind of gun I want.'

Colin was determined to prove himself to Jeanie and make her admit that he had the stuff in him to be thought of as a forty-four caliber man.

Chapter Eight

Shortly before noon, the men gathered in Ma's living room. Only the Kid had not returned and the others sat around the table eating a meal served by the women. Colin had bought the Dragoon, three hundred .44 paper cartridges, powder, lead for moulding bullets, percussion caps and the old Ranger's gunbelt. This like the revolver, was in good condition, the holster well shaped for a fast twist hand draw. However certain alterations were needed to make it fit Colin and the town's saddler agreed to make the necessary adjustments. Not wishing Jeanie to see the gun until he was competent in its use, Colin had left it at the store.

On their return, Dusty and Colin had learned that Kenny was sleeping comfortably. Ma looked worried as she told them, for she knew that her son would be unfit to ride for some time to come. Nor could he be moved around in the wagon. Guessing what troubled her, Dusty waited for the opportunity to offer any help she might require. Ma's pride would prevent her from asking outright, as he knew, and his own offer must be timed and worded correctly or meet with refusal.

The Kid entered the room and halted to study the other men as they sat around the table.

'It's just about what I'd expect,' he growled. 'All the white folks sat filling their bellies while this poor lil Injun boy's been working.'

'*You've* been working?' Mark asked. 'Well, they

do say there's a time and place for everything.'

'What'd you find out?' Dusty inquired before the Kid could think up an answer suitable for mixed company.

'Arnie lit out just a mite after the shooting,' the Kid replied. 'I was going to try looking for him, but figured I'd best tell you first.'

'Any chance of you finding him?' Dusty wanted to know.

'Not a whole heap,' admitted the Kid. 'He took off along the trail, could've left it anywhere. Happen *Ka-Dih's* willing, I'll cut his sign.'

'Forget it,' Dusty decided. 'We'll let them make the next move.'

'They may not try,' Colin put in.

'They'll try,' Mark told him.

'There's nothing more sure than that,' the Kid agreed. 'Now Vicente's gone under, they've got to cut you down.'

'Then I'll go back to the hotel,' Colin stated and started to rise.

'The hell you will!' Ma snapped. 'You're staying with us.'

'We stand a better chance of licking them if we're all together,' Dusty went on. 'If we split up, they can pick us off one at a time.'

'Dusty can look after you better if you stay here,' Jeanie remarked.

'Damn it!' Colin barked, slamming a hand on to the table. 'I'm not a child to need looking after. And I'm asking no man to fight for me.'

'And I'm not offering to,' Dusty said quietly, giving Jeanie a glare which made her squirm in her seat. 'This's not just your fight, Colin. Lou and Miss Hosman each killed one of the gang. Lon downed two. I shot another of them. That means the Flores gang'll be after all of us. So we've go to stand together.'

'Like us *Pehnane* say,' the Kid went on. 'United we stand, divided the Kaddo take our scalps.'

'You're sure that's an old Indian saying?' April

smiled. 'I learned it in school.'

'You white folks're allus taking the red brother's land,' grinned the Kid. 'Looks like you're wide-looping his sayings now.'

That broke the air of tension. Sinking back into his chair, Colin relaxed. He looked at Jeanie, but she turned her face from him.

'I've got to go see that Army hoss buyer this afternoon, Dusty,' Ma said.

'I'll go with you,' Dusty promised. 'On the way back, Colin and I'll pick up our gear from the hotel.'

'You'd best bring your things from the Black Bear, April,' Ma went on.

'Thanks, Ma,' April replied. 'Only what'll your neighbours say when they hear you've got me staying with you?'

'Nothing to me,' Ma grinned. 'And what I don't hear 'em say won't make me lose sleep.'

'You can maybe make some arrangements with your boss about working,' Dusty told the blonde. 'Couple of us'll go with you and see you safe back here.'

'If you're looking for volunteers——' Mark began hopefully.

'Put me down top of the list,' Temple interrupted. 'Depot agent allows I'd best not take any stages out until this blows over.'

'You and Lou go help Miss Hosman move in, Mark,' Dusty decided. 'Colin and me'll be with you, Ma. Reckon you can hold the house if I leave Lon to do the heavy toting, Jeanie?'

'I'll make a whirl at it,' the girl replied.

So the matter was decided. The men finished their meal and the two parties left the house. Neither Dusty nor Mark carried his Winchester, but Temple toted his Spencer. On reaching the main street, April went with her escort to the saloon. Ma, Dusty and Colin made their way towards the hotel. People on the sidewalk eyed the young Scot with interest. There was the man who had killed two of the Flores brothers. One topic of conversation ran through Fort

Sawyer; how much longer would Colin Farquharson live.

Two horsemen galloped along the street as Dusty's party approached the hotel. Although the small Texan tensed slightly, he soon relaxed when he recognised them. They were the cowhands who had helped to deliver the small herd of cattle to the Army post and their coming solved a problem for him. Up until then he had been wondering how to deliver their property to the Schell house. Bringing their horses to a sliding halt, the cowhands dropped from the saddles. Tall, lean, wiry youngsters, they wore cowhand clothes as if born to them—which they had been—and each carried a low-hanging Army Colt. Going by the names 'Shad' and 'Tex', they had impressed Colin the previous night by their happy-go-lucky natures and loyalty to Dusty Fog.

'Heard about the fuss, Capn' Dusty,' Shad announced, his youthful attempt at a moustache quivering with eagerness.

'We was over to Aunt Emmie's for the night and only just now got the word,' Tex went on, feeling their lack of support called for explanation. 'Where're they at and when do we take 'em?'

'Later, maybe,' Dusty replied. 'Right now I want you to get a buckboard and take our gear around to Ma's place.'

Disappointment flickered on the cowhands' faces, but they nodded and tied their horses to the hotel's hitching rail. Showing an expression of concern, the desk clerk watched Ma and the four men coming to his desk. However relief replaced the concern when he learned that Dusty and Colin planned to leave. It saved him the unpleasant task—passed down by the manager who had departed after doing so—of informing them that their rooms would be required that night for a mythical party of guests. After offering to help remove Dusty's party's property, the clerk told Ma where she could find the Army's horse buyer.

'I'll tend to the gear, Ma,' Dusty suggested.

'Tiburcio Flores's too slick to make fuss for you with an important Army officer here. Come on up and pack your stuff, Colin.'

'I thought the clerk would object to us leaving at such short notice,' Colin remarked as they went to the stairs.

'He's likely pleased to see us go,' Dusty replied. 'If Flores comes, we'll be away from the hotel.'

'Flores seems to have a lot of people worried,' Colin said.

'He has, that's why he's lasted so long,' Dusty answered. 'Keeping people scared's how he stays alive. So he has to get you and the other stage passengers to show folks nobody can kill his kin or men and live to tell about it.'

Going along a passage, Ma knocked at the door of the horse-buyer's room. It was opened by Colonel Monaltrie, whom she knew. Big, hearty, he had the well-padded comfortable look of a professional desk-soldier. Yet Ma knew him to be a shrewd businessman and capable in the matter of horsetrading.

'Ah, Mrs. Schell,' Monaltrie greeted, his voice still retaining a Scottish burr. 'Come in. I was sorry to hear about your husband.'

On entering the room, Ma found it already had an occupant. Sprig Branch slouched in a chair by the table and grinned at her with all amiability of a Mississippi alligator about to engulf a bowfin fish.

'Thanks, Colonel,' Ma said, taking the seat he offered her. 'I hear the Army wants horses.'

'We do,' Monaltrie agreed. 'At least five hundred and as many more as we can get. Geldings mostly, but we'll take mares. Whole colours, not paints. We'll pay ten to thirty dollars a head.'

'Delivered here?' Ma inquired, although the words had been directed at both of them.

'Yes,' Monaltrie agreed. 'But Mr. Branch said that your family had gone out of the mustanging business.'

'I figured you had, Ma,' Branch put in, full of false apology. 'What with Kenny getting shot up and all.'

'Kenny?' the colonel repeated. 'Isn't your son with you, Mrs. Schell?'

'Like Sprig couldn't wait to tell you, he got shot this morning.'

'He's not——'

'No, Colonel. Just wounded. He'll be all right in three-four weeks.'

'I'm afraid we can't wait three or four weeks,' Monaltrie told her. 'Whoever gets the contract must be prepared to start out within forty-eight hours.'

'Me 'n' my boys're ready to go right now,' Branch commented.

'And so are we!' Ma snapped.

'But with Kenny wounded——' Monaltrie began.

'Jeanie and me both know mustanging,' Ma stated. 'We've been out with Trader on all his trips and he taught us all he knew.'

'Now, Colonel,' Branch interjected. 'I'm not doubting Trader taught Ma and Jeanie plenty, or gainsaying there were few could touch him at the mustanging game, but two women-folk can't go out alone after wild hosses.'

'We won't be alone,' Ma replied. 'Our *mesteneros* are waiting for us at——' The words chopped off as she caught a flicker of interest on Branch's face and realised that he would like to know where she planned to hunt. 'Well, they're waiting for us and'll likely have some *mestenas** scouted out by now.'

'Greasers,' Branch grunted. 'You reckon you can trust 'em, two white women out there alone?'

'I can trust them!' Ma stated, but she could see that Branch's point worried Monaltrie. 'Both Jeanie and me've been on our lonesome with them afore now, and separate from each other comes to that.'

'And they knowed that Trader 'n' Kenny was around to tend to their needings if they tried anything,' Branch pointed out. 'This time you'll have no men along.'

'Damn it, I tell you I can trust my *mesteneros*!' Ma

**Mestenas:* Bands of wild horses.

snapped. 'Colonel, we can bring in those horses for you.'

'So can we,' Branch said.

Monaltrie looked from Ma to Branch and back again. Since taking on the duty of Army horse-buyer, he had come to know much about mustangers. All the horses brought in by Trader Schell had been good stock and in fine condition. The same could not be claimed for Branch, whose methods ruined the spirits of many of the mustangs. Some officers claimed that Branch's stock trained easier, but others swore that he produced more than his share of over-nervous mounts, or outlaws no man could tame. If Trader Schell was still alive, there would have been no doubt in Monaltrie's mind—but Trader had died a few months before. Could two women fill the contract?

'I'll have to think it over,' the officer decided. 'If you will come around tonight at eight, I will give you my decision.'

'That's fine with me,' Ma said and Branch could do nothing but agree.

Escorting his guests from the room, Monaltrie saw Colin waiting outside. For a moment the colonel stared, his eyes taking in the young Scot's kilt and lifting to Colin's face.

'*Càrn na cuimhne!*' Monaltrie said, advancing with an outstretched right hand.

'*Càrn na cuimhne!*' Colin replied, although surprised to hear his clan's slogan* from the lips of an officer in the United States Army.

'Lad, it's long since I last saw the Farquharson tartan,' Monaltrie boomed, pumping Colin's hand. 'My name's Douglas Monaltrie, my folks came from Aberdeen.'

'I'm Colin Farquharson of Inverey,' Colin introduced.

'And what brings you to this land, lad?'

'I'm working for Mrs. Schell.'

A low grunt of disbelief broke from Branch and, if

*Slogan: Clan rallying cry meaning 'Cairn of Remembrance'.

he had been looking her way, Monaltrie might have read the surprise that flickered across Ma's face.

'You are, are you?' the colonel said thoughtfully.

'He's only a dude and never been mustanging!' Branch growled indignantly.

'The Farquharsons of Inverey're noted as horsemen,' Monaltrie contradicted. 'Didn't John, the third Laird, the Black Colonel, escape from the Hanoverians by riding up the steep side of the Pass of Ballater?'

'That he did,' Colin agreed. 'I'm no claiming to be his equal, mind, but I've ridden ever since I was a wee lad.'

'And you've come out here to be a mustanger?' Monaltrie asked.

'To learn the business,' Colin agreed. 'The Schell family were recommended highly as the best people to teach it to me.'

'You're with the right folk to learn,' Monaltrie admitted and stood for a moment, looking at the roof. 'Like I said, I'll make my decision and tell you about it at eight this evening.' Then he looked at Colin and went on, 'Will you have dinner with me when I'm through?'

'With pleasure, sir,' Colin replied. 'Unless my boss wants me to work.'

'You and your daughter will be welcome to join us, Mrs. Schell,' Monaltrie invited. 'And you, Mr. Branch.'

'Thanks, colonel,' Ma smiled. 'We'll be here.'

With that they separated. Monaltrie returned to his room, while Branch stalked angrily from the building. Not until she and Colin stood in the hall waiting for Dusty did Ma raise the points which were bothering her.

'How long'd you been listening in the passage?'

'Not listening, Mrs. Schell,' Colin corrected. 'I came to see how long you would be—and the colonel's voice carries well.'

'And how long've you been working for me?'

'Ever since Kenny was shot saving *me*.'

'Monaltrie seemed tolerable took with you.'

'He belongs to my clan,' Colin explained. 'I knew it as soon as he gave the slogan.'

'And you reckon he'll give us the contract because of that?' Ma asked.

'No. But he'll be the more willing now he knows you have a man along,' Colin replied. 'That is, if you'll let me come along.'

'Son,' Ma grinned. 'I'll be pleased to have you—— Only, if we don't get that contract, you'll've lost a job.'

Seething with anger, Branch crossed the street to where he had left his men in a small, dingy bar room. He found them talking with a gangling, hook-nosed man.

'Did you get the contract, Sprig?' Moore inquired.

'What happened?' Eric Trimble went on. 'We saw Ma go in with that Scottish son-of-a-bitch and the fellers from the OD Connected.'

'She was after the contract,' Branch growled. 'Then, turns out that Scotch bastard's kin to Monaltrie and's working for the Schells.'

'So?' Sam Trimble asked.

'Monaltrie's going to think on it and tell us tonight who's getting the contract.'

'You reckon that Scotch cuss might swing it for Ma?' Eric wanted to know.

'He could,' admitted Branch. 'I had Monaltrie going again' Ma 'cause she'd no man along afore the Scot showed.'

'Then let's get rid of him,' Moore suggested.

'Who's this?' Branch snapped, nodding towards the lanky man.

'Hacker Boone,' Moore introduced. 'He wants a riding chore and I told him we'd likely need men.'

For a moment Branch studied the prospective job-seeker. Boone was not a prepossessing person, having a face which told of a vicious, sly nature. However, the mustanger regarded him favourably on those very grounds. Such a man would not be overburdened with scruples, especially when currying favour for a job.

'We won't if we don't get the contract,' Branch stated. ' 'Course, if that Scot warn't around, Monaltrie'd likely find for us.'

'After we've wide-looped one of his kin?' Moore said with as near derision as he dare show.

'Not us,' Branch told the men. 'If anything happens to him, who'll folks blame—The Flores gang.'

'What'll we do, Sprig?' Sam asked.

'Now I'd say that all depends on how bad Hacker here wants to work for me,' Branch replied and outlined his scheme.

Chapter Nine

Leaving the hotel, Ma, Dusty and Colin went to Hoffer's general store. There Ma asked to see the owner in private. From the look on his face, Hoffer guessed at the nature of her business and did not care to discuss it. However, he led Ma into the rear of the building.

A rancher, in town to buy supplies, came over and started talking with Dusty and Colin drifted away from them. Walking around the store, he looked at the goods on display. While standing examining a fishing rod, he saw the front door open and a hook-nosed, gangling man entered.

'You Tam Breda's kin?' Hacker Boone asked, coming to the young Scot's side and holding his voice down.

'Aye. That I am.'

'He's down to the livery barn, asking to see you.'

'I'll be along as soon as——' Colin began.

'Tam got stoved up in an accident,' Boone interrupted, noticing the way Colin looked in Dusty's direction.

'I'll come right away,' Colin decided.

For a moment Colin hesitated. Dusty still appeared to be engrossed in conversation with the rancher, so Colin did not wish to intrude. Turning, the young Scot followed Boone from the store. On the sidewalk, the lanky man said he would go and fetch the doctor, then hurried away. One of Boone's stipulations before agreeing to help with Branch's plan had been that he should take no active part in it.

Concerned about Breda's welfare, Colin started to cross the street towards the barn. He remembered the warnings given by Dusty, Mark and the Kid and wondered if he might be walking into a trap. Yet the man who brought the message was white and the Kid had stated that the Flores gang consisted of Mexicans or half-breeds.

Approaching the open door of the barn, Colin slowed down and looked inside. He saw nothing to alarm him or give warning of danger. Then a low moan rose from the interior and Colin plunged through the door. From the corner of his eye, he saw a shape standing against the wall. Even as he tried to turn, something hissed through the air and crashed on to his head. Lights burst before Colin's eyes, then blackness descended and he crumpled forward to the floor.

'Got him!' Eric Trimble grunted, holstering the revolver with which he had struck the Scot down.

'Grab hold and haul him out back,' his brother ordered, moving from where he had stood and attracted Colin's attention.

Moore rose from inside an empty stall, grinning as he studied the result of his impersonation of an injured man. Darting across, he watched the brothers take hold of Colin's arms. However he was not allowed to stand in idleness.

'Go out back and let Sprig know we've got him,' Sam ordered.

'Sure,' Moore agreed and was about to go when he looked through the door. 'Hell's fire! Dusty Fog's coming this way.'

'What'll we do?' Eric croaked, releasing Colin's arm and showing signs of contemplating flight.

'Stay put!' Sam spat back. 'We'll never get another chance to lay hands on this bastard. Slinky, drag him across there and then hide. You get behind the door, Sam. We'll give Fog what this son-of-a-bitch got.'

Ma's interview did not take long. Almost before

the door closed Hoffer began to tell her his troubles. While everybody wanted to pay with notes-of-hand, the companies who supplied his goods demanded cash not paper promises. Knowing the state of affairs in Texas, Ma could see the storekeeper's point. She made her offer to pay at the completion of the horse-hunt, but Hoffer hesitated and hedged. Giving a shrug, Ma turned and stalked from the room.

'I'm sorry, Mrs. Schell,' Hoffer was saying as he followed Ma into the store. 'But you can see my position——?'

'Sure,' Ma replied, trying to hide her disappointment. 'I'll—Dusty! Where's Colin?'

'Feller come in and told him something,' the rancher explained as Dusty turned to look around. 'Then they went out together.'

Springing across to the window, Dusty looked out. A low curse broke from his lips as he saw Colin was alone and entering the barn. It seemed that the young Scot had forgotten all the floating outfit's warnings and their arrangements. Most likely he was walking into a trap.

'What's up, Dusty?' called the rancher, watching the small Texan leap to and jerk open the door. 'Can I help?'

'Stay out of it, Stormy,' Dusty replied, not wanting his friend to become involved in a fuss with the Flores brothers, and went out fast.

Moving around the counter, Ma crossed the room with some speed. For all that, by the time she reached the sidewalk Dusty was approaching the front of the livery barn. Looking along the street, Ma saw Mark, April and Temple leaving the Black Bear. However she did not wait to attract their attention but followed Dusty.

Alert for trouble or danger, Dusty slowed down as he drew near to the barn's door. Looking inside, he saw Colin sprawled face down on the floor by the stalls. Without drawing his guns, Dusty stepped through the door. He acted as if his full attention was centred on the unconscious Scot. Yet his whole being was at hair-trigger alertness. A slight movement to his right gave warning of a lurking enemy in that direction.

Which was just what the waiting men hoped would happen.

Almost sick with fear, knowing the dangerous nature of their proposed victim, Eric lunged from his place at the left of the door. He swept his revolver around parallel to the ground, aiming it to pass under the brim of Dusty's Stetson and strike the base of the skull. Caught there, the small Texan would be unable to cause them any trouble.

At the last moment Dusty bent his legs and ducked under the revolver. His felt it brush the crown of his hat in passing and prepared to deal with its user. Taken by surprise, Eric continued to move forward. Drawing up and bending his left arm, Dusty propelled its elbow against his attacker's solar plexus. The force of the unexpected blow halted Eric's advance and hurled him backwards. His chest front felt as if it had been caved in and the breath burst from his lungs as he sat down hard.

While dealing with his first assailant, Dusty did not forget to stay alert. He knew the men were not members of the Flores gang, which gave him some small comfort. Without worrying over who they might be, or why they had attacked Colin, he gave the barn a quick scrutiny. A small man rose from concealment in the stall near to where Colin lay and there was that cuss who had attracted Dusty's attention from the right side of the door. Three to one at least. Big odds. However Dusty had one detail in his favour.

Back at the OD Connected, Ole Devil Hardin had a servant thought by most folk to be Chinese. Tommy Okasi was Oriental, but hailed from the Japanese islands, not China. When he came to America, he had brought certain fighting skills from his country and passed them on to the smallest male member of the Hardin, Fog and Blaze clan. Dusty figured his knowledge of *ju-jitsu* and *karate*, all but unknown in the Western Hemisphere, backed by his unexpected strength and rough-house fighting skill gave him something of an edge.

Seeing his brother's attack fail, Sam leapt forward. From striking Eric, Dusty pivoted around. Clenching his fight fist, he avoided Sam's reaching hands. From his left hip, the right arm lashed around in a powerful swing towards Sam's head. The way Dusty used his fist looked awkward to eyes which knew only Western methods, but proved mighty effective. Passing over Sam's reaching hands, the fist met his face. Its protruding second knuckle caught the centre of Sam's top lip hard enough to spin him around and send him stumbling away.

Moore left the stall, to which he had returned after dragging Colin across the barn, and prepared to take cards. With a yell that was three-parts fear, he snatched up a pitchfork that leaned against the side of the stall. Gripping its handle as if using a rifle and bayonet, he moved forward ready to help Sam. When the lanky man failed to deal with Dusty, Moore charged in. As he came into range, he drew back the fork and launched a savage thrust.

From knocking Sam aside, Dusty spun around to meet the fresh danger. Already the sharp twin tines were driving towards his body. Swiftly Dusty twisted himself aside, bringing his right hand down to grasp the pitchfork just below its head. With a savage jerk, he forced the fork outwards and downwards. A wail of shock broke from Moore. Before he could prevent it or halt his attack, the tines spiked into the ground behind his intended victim. Interlacing his fingers, Dusty spun around and crashed them into Moore's back as the man was forced to bend forward. Again Moore howled. The tines snapped under his weight. However the handle of the fork, which he still gripped, acted as a fulcrum. Carried on by his own impetus and the force of Dusty's blow, Moore turned a somersault, passed through the door and lit down on his back in the street.

Through the mists of pain caused by the blow to his lip, Sam saw Dusty's back turn to him and took the chance it offered. Thrusting himself forward, he locked his arms around Dusty's torso from behind. Feeling the surging power of the small Texan's powerful biceps, Sam decided that he needed help.

'Eric!' Sam yelled, swinging Dusty's feet from the floor. 'Help me, damn you. Help me!'

Given that much of an advantage, Eric was only too willing to comply. Sucking in deep gasps of air to re-fill his tormented lungs, he hurled himself towards his brother and the small Texan. Seeing Dusty Fog held in such a vulnerable manner, Eric figured to repay the blow interest.

The trouble was that Dusty did not regard himself as being helpless. Although his arms were pinioned to his sides, the same did not apply to his legs. If anything, being suspended in such a way helped rather than hindered him. Up lashed his right leg, sending the toe of its boot under Eric's jaw. The kick landed hard, flinging him in a spinning line across the barn.

Surging around, Sam flung Dusty from him. Despite landing on his feet, Dusty could not prevent himself from colliding solidly with the wall. Following him up, Sam turned him and crashed a punch to the side of his head. A second blow drove into the hard muscles of Dusty's belly, bringing a grunt of pain. Then Sam's hands clamped hold of his neck. Drawing Dusty forward, Sam slammed him savagely against the wall and the fingers crushed at his throat, threatening to strangle him.

On the street, Moore dragged himself erect. He was so engrossed in his aching body and thoughts of revenge that he was oblivious of his surroundings. Turning, he started to jerk out his revolver as a preliminary to re-entering the barn. As he moved forward, a hand clamped hold of his right shoulder and swung him outwards. To his surprise, he found himself faced with Ma Schell. Releasing the shoulder, she uncorked a round-house swing. Her whole body turned with the punch, adding its weight to the clenched right fist. Being a mustanger's wife was not a sedentary occupation and Ma's buxom frame carried hard muscles. More than that, she knew how to throw a punch. Her knuckles connected solidly on Moore's jaw, snapping his head over and pitching him sideways. From the way he landed, he would not be rising for some time.

Shaking her right hand and making a wry face, Ma summed up the situation. She knew who Moore worked for, so guessed why Colin had been lured into the barn. From various sounds which reached her ears and the lack of gun-shots, she concluded that Dusty was tangling barehanded with more of Branch's men. Most likely he would need help, despite those fancy tricks learned from Tommy Okasi. Which raised the point of how she might best give him assistance.

Ma knew her limitations. Sure she packed a useful punch and had just stretched Slinky Moore on the ground. That did not mean she could achieve similar success against the Trimbles or Sprig Branch. Besides, there was a much better way to help the small Texan.

Turning to look in the direction of the Black Bear, she saw no sign of Mark Counter's party. Most likely they had not noticed Dusty cross to the barn, so turned along an alley with the intention of returning to Ma's house. Giving a low snort, Ma expanded her lungs and cut loose with a yell that rang along the street.

'Mark! Mark Counter! Dusty's needing help!'

A point with which Dusty was in agreement. Only he did not figure on waiting until somebody came to give it to him. Sam's fingers closed on his throat and the man drew him forward for another crash into the wall. Something had to be done, and fast.

Although unable to prevent it, Dusty managed to brace himself and reduce the impact of his collision with the wall. Then he struck back. To obtain a better grip, Sam had raised and spread his arms from his sides. So he presented Dusty with a way of getting free. Once again the small Texan attacked as Tommy

Okasi had taught him. With his fingers extended and thumbs bent over the up-turned palms, he chopped the heels of his hands suddenly and savagely into the sides of Sam's short ribs. The result of the attack was devastating to its recipient. Sam's eyes bugged out, his mouth trailed open and worked in soundless agony. Opening involuntarily, his hands left Dusty's throat and fell limply to his sides.

The rear door of the barn flew open and Sprig Branch came in. Fury twisted his face at what he saw, He had never hoped to be so lucky as to grab Colin in such an easy manner. He had seen Ma's party enter the general store and sent Boone to watch for an opportunity to lure the Scot away, then stationed his men in the empty barn—its owner and staff being at the Black Bear Saloon—in case a chance arose. It came, but Dusty Fog's intervention might ruin everything. Like Sam, Branch realised they would not have another opportunity to remove Colin. So the mustanger did not mean to let it slip by.

Looking across the barn, Branch saw Eric lurch to his brother's assistance and advanced meaning to help him. A groan brought Branch's eyes to Colin as the Scot tried to force himself on to his hands and knees. All the mustanger's fury broke in full force at the sight. Maybe he would lose the contract, but he aimed to make sure that Ma Schell did not get it through Colin's help. Changing his direction, he went towards Colin.

Freed from Sam's grasp by the *tegatana*, hand-sword, attack, Dusty went on to show that he could fight in Occidental fashion. His right fist ripped into Sam's belly, jackknifing the other over. Coming up, Dusty's knee met the descending face with a sickening thud. Lifted erect, blood spraying from his nose, Sam reeled away from Dusty and fell dazed to the floor.

Arriving just as his brother took the knee in the face, Eric caught hold of Dusty by the front of his shirt and vest. Having no desire to tangle at close quarters with the deadly-fighting *big* Texan, Eric exerted all his strength to heave and hurl Dusty across the barn. He hoped to be able to draw and use a weapon before Dusty could come to a stop, then return to the attack.

Going forward, Dusty saw Branch looming beyond the helpless Colin and drawing back a foot to deliver a kick. So Dusty did not try to stop himself. Instead he used Eric's heave to build up momentum that would help to save the Scot. Springing from the floor, Dusty cleared Colin's body. In midair, rushing towards Branch, he bent and drew up his legs. Then he thrust them forward, crashing his feet into the mustanger's chest. Coming as Branch stood balanced on one leg, the leaping high kick landed with sufficient force to lift him off the ground and hurl him backwards so that he collided hard against the end of the nearest stall's wall.

Behind Dusty, Eric jerked the knife from his belt. Again caution prevented him from going too close. Instead he whipped up his arm, ready to throw the weapon at the small Texan's back. Realising the lanky man's intention as she entered the barn, Ma saw also the means of countering it. Bending, she scooped up the handle of the pitchfork discarded by Moore. Even as Eric's arm rose into the air, Ma gripped and swung the handle in both hands. Hissing round in a whistling arc, the handle descended on to Eric's skull and splintered. Although the knife left his hand, it flew wild and spiked into a bale of hay. Buckling at the knees, Eric collapsed in a limp heap.

Bouncing forward uncontrolled, Branch ran into more trouble. Dusty landed from the kick and reacted almost instinctively as he saw the mustanger coming his way. Catching the dazed man's right arm at the wrist and shoulder, he pivoted into a *kata-seoi* shoulder throw, Bowing his legs, Dusty used Branch's weight and impetus to catapult the man over his shoulder. Passing above Colin, Branch crashed awkwardly to the floor.

Feet thudded on the street and Mark Counter burst

into the barn with his right-hand Colt held ready for use. Skidding to a halt, the blond giant looked around. Then he turned to Ma, dropping the gun back into its holster.

'I thought you yelled that Dusty was in trouble,' Mark said.

'You're too late,' Ma replied. 'We settled everything for ourselves.'

'You all right, *amigo*?' Mark inquired of Dusty, while Ma went across to Colin.

Sucking in a deep breath, Dusty touched the side of his jaw. Then he nodded and replied, 'Sure.'

Among the people attracted by the disturbance, Colonel Monaltrie made his way to the barn. Coming through the door, he stared about him.

'What the——' he began.

'Branch and his bunch tricked Colin into coming here and jumped him,' Ma explained, helping the young Scot to turn into a sitting position.

Before any more could be said, the sheriff arrived. Finding a U.S. Army colonel present, and one who probably had more influence even than the local post commanding officer, Lansing prepared to show greater zeal than he normally employed in the execution of his duty. Glaring around, he took in the sight of Ma kneeling alongside Colin and Branch's men scattered about the barn. Putting a brisk, efficient note into his voice, Lansing demanded to be told what had happened. So Dusty repeated the information Ma had given to Monaltrie.

'Why'd Sprig Branch do that?' Lansing asked. 'It ain't likely he's working for the Flores boys.'

'Why should Branch be working for the Flores gang?' Monaltrie inquired, turning back towards the sheriff instead of joining Ma and Colin.

'I ain't saying he is,' Lansing protested. 'Only there don't seem to be no other reason for him jumping that young feller.'

'So it was Colin there who killed Adán Flores in the holdup,' the colonel breathed. 'And shot the other one in the street. I thought somebody was jobbing me when I heard it had been done by a Scot wearing a kilt.'

'It's the living truth,' Dusty confirmed. 'Which's likely why Branch figured he could get away with making Colin disappear. Folks'd blame it on the Flores boys and it'd leave Ma without a man.'

'You reckon that's what's behind it, Cap'n Fog?' Lansing inquired.

'It figures,' Dusty answered. 'Maybe they'll feel like telling you when they get to talking.'

'Will I be needed?' asked the town's doctor, entering the barn with his bag.

'Not here,' Ma replied, helping Colin to rise. 'He's got a knot on his head, but nothing's cut or busted.'

'You'd best take a look at Branch,' Dusty suggested. 'He lit down kind of awkward.'

Taking the advice, the doctor crossed and knelt down by Branch. Nobody spoke as he made an examination of the unconscious man. At last he raised a startled face towards the on-lookers.

'I'll say he lit down awkward. His collarbone's bust. And what the hell kicked him? He's got three broken ribs.'

Sucking in a deep breath, Monaltrie let it out again in an exasperated exclamation. A man in Branch's condition could not go mustang-hunting. Which meant that, unless the colonel wanted to wait until other mustangers could be contacted and gathered, only the Schell family was available. He wondered if two women and a young man freshly arrived in Texas could fill the contract, even backed by experienced Mexican *mesteneros*.

Chapter Ten

Following his usual way, Sheriff Lansing adopted the line of least resistance. He had no desire to antagonise a man with Dusty's powerful connections, so gave his opinion that the whole blame for the trouble rested on Branch. When Dusty declined to swear out a complaint, Lansing willingly agreed to let the affair be forgotten and promised to make sure that Branch's men caused no more incidents.

After ensuring that Colin had suffered no serious injury, Colonel Monaltrie left the barn. He wanted to think over his future actions before reaching a decision on whether to give Ma the contract.

Picking up Colin's bonnet, Mark handed it to him. Although swaying a little, the young Scot refused help and walked outside with the others. They found April and Temple waiting and the whole group started to walk across the street.

'Did you fix up about working tonight?' Ma asked the blond.

'It didn't need any fixing,' April replied wryly. 'When Harve Jute arrived, he fired me.'

'Why?' Ma demanded.

'He's scared. Reckons that with the Flores bunch after me his place's likely to get shot up and paying customers killed. More likely he thinks the customers'll stay away.'

'I'll go down and see him,' Dusty growled and Mark rumbled agreement.

'It won't do any good at all,' April assured him. 'I

only just got Mark and this old goat——'

'She means me,' Temple interrupted.

'Who else, damn it?' April snorted. 'They were all set to hang Harve's saloon around his neck and I only just managed to get them out afore they started. Did you ever try talking sense to a man, Ma?'

'Allus found whomping 'em with a hickory bar worked better,' Ma grinned.

'I should've had one to hand,' April stated. 'It's lucky you yelled when you did, or they'd still've gone back to do it.'

'What'll you do now, gal?' Ma inquired.

April shrugged. 'I've been fired out of better places than the Black Bear. There're other saloons.'

'Not in Fort Sawyer,' Dusty warned. 'The word'll've gone out about you.'

'So there're other towns,' April sniffed.

' 'Cepting that when you try to go to one, the Flores boys'll be waiting for you,' Mark warned.

'You're welcome to stay on with us, April gal,' Ma announced. 'Maybe Lansing or the Army'll get around to doing something about those Flores critters real soon.'

'If they don't, I aim to,' Dusty promised, before April could express her gratitude. 'Soon's we get to the house, I'm going to send Lon out on a scout for their hideout.'

'Won't that be dangerous?' Colin asked.

'Real dangerous,' Mark agreed. 'For Flores and his *bandidos*.'

While the others were talking, Ma had been looking at Dusty with worried eyes. Taking a deep breath, she made a decision. With Branch out of the game and Colin acceptable to Monaltrie as a protecting male influence, she stood a good chance of receiving the Army contract. Yet she could not fill it without supplies and Hoffer wanted cash for them. Ma had her fair share of pride and her brother-in-law's behaviour made her fight shy of asking favours. Accepting there was no other way out, she set her face into impassive lines and moved to the small Texan's side.

'Can I have a few words with you up to the house, Dusty?' she asked.

'Why sure, Ma,' Dusty replied, guessing what the topic of conversation would be. 'Any old time at all.'

The Schell house had been erected on the edge of town and clear of other buildings. Behind it stood their wagon, canopy removed for loading and empty. The team horses shared a corral at the right of the building with Jeanie's coyote-dun mare and Kenny's powerful grulla gelding. Curving around from the left, a large *bosque* stretched to the rear of the house. However an open area of not less than seventy yards separated the building from the trees. Although the hotel's buckboard was hitched before the porch, it had been unloaded and was deserted.

'I sure hope you've plenty of chow in, Ma,' Mark commented as they walked towards the building. 'That Shad and Tex'll eat——'

A shot crashed from among the trees, its bullet slashing in front of Dusty and Ma to tear into Temple's chest. Giving a choking cry, the driver reeled, let his carbine fall from the crook of his arm and crumpled to the ground. On the heels of the shot, riders burst out of the *bosque*. They were Mexicans holding guns and they charged towards Dusty's party.

'Down!' Dusty roared, hands crossing in flickers of movement so that the bark of his left-side Colt echoed the word.

Living in frontier Texas had taught Ma to react instantly in such a situation. So she was diving for the ground almost before Dusty spoke. No less quick to appreciate the danger, April followed Ma down. Bringing out his Colts, Mark remained standing and cut loose at the attacking *bandidos*.

Like Dusty and Mark, Colin stayed on his feet. Bullets hissed around the Scot and he realised that the gang were concentrating their fire on him. Fury filled him as he decided that the first shot had been meant for him, but missed and killed Lou Temple. At the same moment, Colin became aware that he did not have a weapon. The alterations to the gunbelt had not been completed and the Dragoon was still at the store, while his shot-pistols had been left behind with his other belongings to be moved to Ma's house.

Then Colin saw Temple's Spencer. Bending for it, he missed death by inches as a bullet passed just above his lowered head. Grabbing up the carbine, he sprang over Ma and April to sprint away from the house. In doing so, he hoped to draw the *bandidos'* fire and attack after him, clear of his friends.

The intention paid off. Seeing the man who had killed his brothers running towards the town, Matteo Flores swung towards him. Followed by the majority of the attackers, the stocky *bandido* thundered after Colin. Matteo drew ahead of the others, holding his fire until sure that he could not miss.

When lead started to splatter close around him, Colin knew he must run no more. If he was to die, he meant to go out as a Highlander, facing his enemies and fighting. So he slammed to a halt, pivoted around and snapped the carbine to his shoulder. There would be no time to take a careful bead. Colin looked along the barrel rather than making use of the sights, seeing the stocky, villainous shape of Matteo looming closer at the head of the attackers. An instant ahead of the Dragoon, the Spencer bellowed. As the carbine spoke, Matteo's horse jerked its head up into the line of the shot. A .52 bullet struck the horse's skull and it started to crumple forward on its buckling legs. Feeling his horse going down, Matteo also saw his shot churn up dirt between the Scot's feet. A born horseman, Matteo kicked free his feet and quit the falling animal's back. At the same moment he realised that the attack was a failure.

Leaving Mark to take on the four or so men coming their way, Dusty turned his attention to Colin's pursuers. Left, right, left right, the small Texan's long-barrelled Army Colts sent lead at

Matteo's men. One rider screamed and slid sideways from his horse. Another cried out, swaying in his saddle. Bursting from the house, the Kid, Shad and Tex added their volume of fire to their companions'. Mark tumbled a man over the rump of his mount. Another was aiming at the blond giant when a flat-nosed .44 Winchester bullet ripped into his head.

Human flesh could only stand such treatment for a short time. Showing superb riding skill, the remaining *bandidos* spun their horses around and fled. Matteo was no fool. On foot, he was in great danger, an easier target than a mounted moving man and with less chance of escape. So he did not hesitate. There would be other times when revenge could be had on the man in the skirt. Matteo knew that the family honour demanded the man should die, but had no intention of being killed while doing it. Bounding on to the horse of the man Dusty had shot, Matteo whirled it in a rump-scraping turn. Swinging over to hang on the flank of the horse farthest from the house, Matteo followed his fleeing companions towards the *bosque*.

'Head for the house, Ma!' Dusty snapped. 'Get after 'em, Lon!'

'Yo!' the black-dressed youngster replied.

Jeanie came from the house carrying the Sharps, shotgun and her father's Henry rifle. Ignoring the sight of the men moving towards the *bosque*, she carried her burden over to where her mother and April had started to stand up.

'What happened?' the girl asked, handing the weapons out.

'Colin just saved our lives,' Ma replied. 'If he hadn't run——'

'*Run?*' Jeanie ejaculated.

'Let me finish!' Ma snapped. 'If he hadn't run down there and drawn them after him, they'd've rid clear over us.'

Holding the Sharps carbine, Jeanie turned to look to where Colin had entered the *bosque* with the other men. Maybe there was more to him than she had first imagined. She gave a sniff. Not that she cared one way or another, of course. With that point settled, she turned her attention back to her mother. Ma and April knelt at Temple's side. Looking at the wound, they exchanged glances. There was nothing anybody but the undertaker could do.

Fanning out among the trees, Dusty's party advanced. At first they had the noise of the *bandidos*' hurried passage to guide them. Then it ended, but hooves drummed off across the range beyond the *bosque*. For all that, Dusty kept his men moving. In addition to remaining alert, Dusty took the opportunity to see how Colin reacted. Clearly the Scot had done considerable hunting. Colin moved carefully and without undue noise. Carrying the carbine ready for use, he searched every piece of cover ahead of him. Grim determination showed on the Scot's face, along with another emotion Dusty could not decipher.

The men passed through the *bosque* without incident. On its outer side, they saw the *bandidos* galloping away in the distance.

'You want for us to take out after 'em, Dusty?' asked the Kid, and the two cowhands listened hopefully at his side.

'Not right now,' Dusty replied. 'Was that the full gang?'

'Not more'n half I'd say,' the Kid answered. 'Fifteen at most. Didn't see Tiburcio along, or Matteo comes to that.'

Remembering the appearance of the other two brothers, Colin did not connect the stocky, poorly-dressed Matteo with them and so said nothing.

'Don't seem likely the gang'd come without one of 'em along,' Mark objected.

'You boys'd best search this *bosque* extra careful,' Dusty decided, for he agreed with Mark. 'Go to it. You'd best come back to the house with me, Colin. There could be another try and the women-folk're alone.'

'Aye,' Colin answered.

Leaving Mark, the Kid, Shad and Tex to conduct the search, Dusty returned with Colin through the *bosque*. As they walked, Colin turned his face towards Dusty and let out a long sigh.

'I should never have come to Texas,' the Scot announced. 'None of this would be happening then.'

'Maybe,' Dusty replied.

'Kenny wouldn't have been wounded,' Colin continued. 'And Lou Temple would still be alive. Lou was killed because of me.'

'How'd you figure that out?' Dusty asked.

'That bullet was meant for me, the one that hit him.'

'Nope,' contradicted Dusty. 'It was fired from a rifle and aimed at Lou.'

'How can you be sure?'

'Lou was toting that Spencer. So he was the biggest danger to 'em when they first showed from here in the trees. Figuring that, they took him out of the game first.'

'Do you think that's true?' Colin asked eagerly.

'I'd bet on it,' Dusty assured him. 'And what you did was mighty brave. Going away from us like that took guts.'

'Or I was in a panic,' Colin suggested.

'The hell you were!' Dusty replied. 'You didn't run scared, you was thinking all the time.'

The droop left Colin's shoulders and he seemed much relieved at Dusty's answer. Up until that moment, Colin had assumed that Dusty and the others would hold him responsible for Temple's death or think he had fled in fright.

Leaving the *bosque*, Colin came to a halt and stared ahead of him. Jeanie and April stood by Temple's body, each holding a weapon. Five *bandidos* sprawled limp and motionless before the house, along with the horse Colin had killed. People were coming from the town, with Lansing and two of his deputies in the lead. Hearing the sound of approaching horses, Colin turned and saw a party of soldiers coming towards them.

'Lou's dead,' April said in a dull voice as the two young men came up.

'They paid dear for it,' Dusty answered, glancing at the bodies. 'Where's Ma at?'

'Gone in to settle Kenny down,' Jeanie replied.

Before any more could be said, the soldiers arrived. Led by a young lieutenant, they were armed with Springfield carbines, revolvers and sabres and looked to be about twenty strong. Halting his men, the lieutenant rode to where Dusty's party stood by Temple's body.

'Was it the Flores gang?' the officer demanded.

'Sure,' Dusty replied. 'They took off through the *bosque* and were still running when we got to the other side.'

'We'll keep them running, unless they're foolish enough to show fight,' the lieutenant stated. 'Troop——'

'I've got a feller who can read sign real good, mister,' Dusty put in, seeing that the soldiers did not have a scout along. 'If you'd like for hi——'

'That won't be necessary. We can handle it,' the officer answered and started to swing his horse away.

'*Mister!*' Dusty barked and something in his tone brought the soldier to an instant halt. 'I've got men searching the woods. Watch out for them.'

For a moment the lieutenant stared down, wondering how he had come to think of Dusty as a small, insignificant man. There was an air of command, a hard-bitten do-it-or-else air about the *big* Texan gained only by a few of the best combat-tried captains and senior ranks. The word 'mister' had cracked out in the manner of such an officer giving a warning to a junior and expecting it to be obeyed. Discipline prevented the lieutenant from raising objections.

'We'll go around the *bosque* and take up the trail at the other side,' he announced. 'Troops, left in threes, ho!'

'Damned shavetail!' Dusty snorted, watching the soldiers depart. 'No scout and he still allows to run the Flores gang down.'

'Will they fight?' Colin asked.

'Not unless they're cornered.' Dusty guessed. 'More likely they'll hide up someplace and let the soldiers hunt for them. Let's see what the sheriff aims to do.'

It quickly became obvious that the sheriff meant to do as little as possible. Using the army's participation as an excuse not to take out a posse, he arranged for the removal of the bodies. Only the local undertaker of the gathered citizens came forward with the sheriff. The other people hovered in the background, talking among themselves. After conferring with the undertaker, Lansing darted a worried glance in Dusty's direction, then turned to April and Colin.

'How much longer will you be in town?' the sheriff asked.

'Until they can leave safely,' Dusty put in. 'Or are you fixing to run them out?'

'Naw!' Lansing stated hurriedly. 'It's only that folk're getting concerned about all this gun-play. Somebody could get hurt.'

'Somebody did!' April snapped, pointing to Temple's body.

'It might be some harmless by-stander next time,' Lansing croaked. 'The Flores bunch won't give up on you.'

Standing at the door of the house, Ma had caught the last part of the conversation and guessed at the rest. Stalking forward, she faced Lansing with grim annoyance on her face.

'Don't let it worry you, sheriff!' she hissed. 'We'll be out of your town afore sundown tomorrow.'

'I ain't pressing you to go, mind!' Lansing whined, flashing worried looks at Dusty. 'Only——'

'You don't have to go, Ma,' Colin put in. 'I will.'

'We're all going!' Ma insisted. 'Even if I have to take a hickory bar to make you come along. Can I have that word with you now, Dusty?'

'My pleasure, ma'am,' Dusty replied. 'That satisfy you, sheriff?'

'Sure—— Well, if Ma's set on going I'll not stop her.'

A harsh guffaw broke from the undertaker, who harboured few illusions about Lansing. 'I bet you won't,' he said. 'Reckon I'll tend to Lou first and move the rest of 'em on the buckboard there.'

Sensing that her mother wanted to speak privately to Dusty, Jeanie suggested that April and Colin should accompany her into the house.

'Best give Colin some of your pa's pick-up medicine, gal,' Ma said. 'He could likely use it.'

'I'm feeling a mite peaked myself,' April commented. 'So I'll try some while you're at it, Jeanie.'

Walking away from the sheriff and undertaker, Ma wondered how she should word her request. The need did not arise.

'How much do you need, Ma?' Dusty asked quietly.

'You knew, huh?' she said.

'I guessed. You'll need supplies if you get the remount contract and Hoffer's having to ask for cash for them.'

'That's about the size of it,' Ma admitted. 'I reckon I can't blame him.'

'Tell me how much you need,' Dusty said, 'and I'll make you out a draft against the Polveroso City bank. I reckon Hoffer'll take it.'

'I—I——' Ma began huskily.

'Uncle Devil'd have my hide if I didn't,' Dusty smiled. 'Don't forget that we need hosses as well as the Army and we'd sooner deal with you Schells than any other mustangers.'

'Th—Thanks, Dusty,' Ma said, blinking her eyes. 'Must've caught a chill.'

'Trader's pick-up medicine's good for that,' Dusty told her, then saw a familiar figure approaching. 'Here's that desk-warming Yankee Colonel. Let's see what he's got to say.'

Coming up, Monaltrie studied the scene and then turned his attention to Ma. 'Are they the Flores gang?'

'Sure,' Dusty answered.

'The whole gang?' Monaltrie said.

'Nope, some of them got away.'

'Did you get the brothers?'

'We didn't even see them,' Dusty admitted.

'Then they'll try again,' Monaltrie remarked.

'It's likely, colonel,' Dusty admitted. 'They can't quit now or they'll never get men to follow them.'

'Damn it!' Monaltrie barked. 'That means they'd be after you when you leave to catch the horses, Mrs. Schell.'

'Sure,' Ma agreed. 'We're going anyways.'

'With young Farquharson?'

'He's one of us now,' Ma stated. 'His fight's our fight. I wouldn't leave him behind even if taking him means I don't get your contract.'

'I intended to give it to you,' Monaltrie told her. 'But with the Flores gang after you and only one white man along——'

'You didn't count right, colonel,' Dusty interrupted. 'There won't be just one white man along.'

'How's that?' Monaltrie asked hopefully.

'Happen Ma'll have us, Mark, the Kid and me'll be going with her,' Dusty replied.

Chapter Eleven

'If anybody'd told me afore I left Galveston that I'd wind up riding on a wagon dressed like this and headed for the Lord only knows where,' April Hosman stated, wriggling in an attempt to find a more comfortable position, 'I'd've spit right in their eye.'

Handling the reins of the powerful six-horse team with deft ease, Ma turned and grinned at the blonde. They both wore Stetson hats, men's shirts, levis pants and boots. While Ma was used to such attire when travelling, April had expressed some dismay on discovering she would be expected to dress that way.

'What's up, gal?' Ma grinned.

'Nothing, except that I look like hell, feel worse and wish I'd stayed in Fort Sawyer and let the Flores boys shoot me. At least I'd've died pretty and quick. This way, I'll be pounded to death from the seat up.'

Ma chuckled. 'Comes another day or two, you'll have callouses so thick on your butt-end you'll not feel the bumps.'

'Callouses on the butt-end's the last thing I need,' April groaned. 'Do you reckon they're after us yet, Ma?'

'If they are, the Kid'll see them,' Ma replied. 'With luck, they don't even know we've gone yet.'

On hearing Dusty's intention to accompany the mustang-hunt, Colonel Monaltrie had forgotten all his misgivings and awarded the contract to the Schell family. After which, things had started to move fast.

At Ma's request, Dusty had taken command and given April—for one—an insight as to how he gained his Civil War reputation. Courage alone had not given Dusty his successes, for he always planned and took advantage of any opportunity which arose.

Knowing that the cavalry patrol would drive the Flores gang out of the immediate vicinity of the town, Dusty stated that they would leave as soon as possible. After which, he had put everybody to work. Accompanied by Mark, Ma visited the store and presented Dusty's bank draft. Hoffer accepted it without argument, knowing that it would be met, and gave willing cooperation to Ma's demands. At the house, Jeanie had seen to packing their belongings ready to leave.

Going to the Army post with Monaltrie, Dusty had interviewed its commanding officer. Colonel Shieling had agreed to have Kenny in the post hospital, where he would be safe from Flores' vengeance until well enough to travel. Although Dusty's other request had been a mite unorthodox, Shieling went along with it. Acting on 'information received', Arnie Hogan was arrested as a suspected deserter; to be held for 'investigation' and ensure that he could pass no further information to the *bandidos*. In that, Hogan might have counted himself fortunate. The Kid had suggested a simpler and more permanent way of achieving the informer's silence, stating his willingness to attend to the matter.

After sun-down, the wagon had been loaded and its team hitched. A protesting Kenny was taken to the post hospital and the party prepared to move out. Much to their disgust, Shad and Tex were told to return to the OD Connected and inform Ole Devil Hardin of Dusty's plans. An empty wagon which looked much like the Schells' Conestoga and eight horses had been borrowed from the owner of the livery barn, to be left at the house for a few days to induce the notion that Ma's party were still there.

Leaving the Kid behind, Dusty led the others out of town in the darkness. The Kid remained at the house until morning. Then he made a circle of the town without finding signs that the *bandidos* had returned and set off after his companions.

With four days between them and Fort Sawyer, there had still been nothing to show that the Flores gang was following them. Not that Dusty took chances. While he and Mark rode out on the flanks, the Kid brought up the rear. Ma and April rode the wagon, leaving the handling of the small remuda to Jeanie and Colin.

Riding along at the rear of the ten spare saddle-horses, Jeanie looked from the corner of her eye at Colin. Over the past four days, with the Texans away on the sky-line most of the time, she had been thrown into the Scot's company as they kept the remuda together. Looking at him, she felt the usual tangle of emotions which always filled her in his presence.

Jeanie could not explain her feelings. While part of her sought for Colin's good points, another part saw only his failings. Sure he had acted bravely during the attack, but before that he had walked into a trap from which Dusty Fog and her mother had rescued him. Despite his outlandish clothes—he still wore his bonnet, shirt and kilt—he rode well. Yet he lacked knowledge of things any Texas boy learned afore his tenth birthday. Sniffing disdainfully, Jeanie recalled how she had had to show him how to hitch up the wagon team and overheard him asking Dusty's advice about saddling the horse allocated to him. She did not take into account that the Texas range kak might differ from the saddles to which Colin was accustomed.

'He's such a greenhorn!' Jeanie mused. 'Not that I care one way or another.'

Conscious of the girl's scrutiny, Colin made no attempt to address her. At first during the journey he had tried to talk with her, but the conversational attempts were received so coldly that he stopped them. Jeanie's attitude hurt him more than he cared to admit, even to himself. However he gritted his teeth and promised silently to prove he was as much of a man as any of the Texans. The Dragoon hung at his side, but he was becoming less aware of it with each passing day. Not that he was allowed to forget it. Each evening on making camp, Dusty, Mark or the Kid would give him instruction in gun-handling. Accuracy with the sights was no problem and he found himself able to plant his bullets close enough to where he wanted them at up to thirty yards range. Drawing and shooting by instinctive alignment would take longer to master, yet his teachers expressed satisfaction with his progress.

Sitting relaxed in his bay gelding's saddle, Colin looked around him. They were travelling across rolling country without as much as a set of wheel ruts to guide them. Yet Ma clearly knew where they were going, even though Colin could hardly tell one fold of land from another. Wondering if he would attain a similar skill if he remained in Texas, Colin turned his eyes towards where Mark Counter appeared on a distant rim. A yell from Jeanie jolted the young Scot out of his reverie.

'Over there!' the girl shouted, pointing to Colin's right.

Following the direction she indicated, he saw a horse coming from a clump of bushes. Colin had rarely seen such a fine animal and so stared at it with admiring gaze. Letting out a shrill whistling whinny, the horse ran forward. With its mane and tail flying in the breeze, it came closer. Snorts broke from the remuda and the bay under Colin fiddle-footed restlessly.

'He's after the remuda!' Ma yelled. 'Head him off, Colin!'

Snatching the rope from his saddle, Colin urged his mount towards the stallion. Although the bay usually responded promptly to commands, it showed some reluctance to obey. Kicking its ribs, he started it moving. Behind him, Jeanie yelled something but Colin could not catch the words.

Nearer thundered the stallion, until it seemed certain to collide with the bay. At the last moment, while the bay fought to turn away, the stallion swung aside. Seeing it start to go by, Colin flipped his rope out. Pure luck guided the noose, dropping over the stallion's head and down its sleek neck. Remembering what Dusty had said the previous night when discussing roping, Colin knew he must secure his lariat before the noose snapped tight. Swift he thew a couple of turns of rope around the horn. Only just in time, for the rope snapped tight between the bay and stallion and tore from his grasp.

Coming around the remuda to help drive off the stallion, Jeanie stared in amazement at what she saw. She also knew the danger of Colin's actions. Jerking the Sharps carbine from its boot, she cut loose from the mare's back and hoped that she would be in time to save the Scot from the results of his folly.

The force of the stallion slamming to the end of the rope almost jerked the bay from its feet. Instantly the wild horse came around in a rearing, sky-pawing turn. Screaming in fury, it laid back its ears and bared its teeth. More experienced than its rider, the bay knew what to expect. As the stallion charged, the bay began a bucking, pitching evasion. Taken by surprise, Colin lost his seat and tumbled to the ground. Desperately he rolled over, hearing the stallion's teeth chop together above him. The stamping forefeet missed him by inches and he continued to roll as the raging horse began to turn for another attack.

Dropping to her left knee, Jeanie flung the carbine into the firing position. Raw anxiety gnawed at her, but she refused to let it fluster her. Making sure of her aim, she squeezed the trigger. Flying true, the heavy bullet struck and broke the stallion's neck. Down it went in a kicking, thrashing pile close to where Colin stopped rolling.

Jeanie had no time to congratulate herself on a good shot. Leaping to her feet, she ran to the mare. Already the remuda had started to flee, fear of the stallion combining with the sound of the shot to set them going. Catching hold of the saddle-horn, she swung afork her horse and sent it bounding after them. Reaction set in as she rode and her temper rose to boiling point at the thought of Colin's behaviour. Once more the Scot's stupidity was making trouble.

Bringing the wagon to a halt, Ma leapt agilely off the box. Followed by April, she dashed across to where Colin sat up and looked around in a dazed manner.

'Are you all right?' April asked.

'I think so,' Colin answered.

'You won't be if you pull another fool trick like that,' Ma warned. 'If Jeanie had moved a mite slower——'

'Aye!' Colin said soberly.

'Come on,' Ma ordered as the Scot stood up. 'Get your rope off the stallion and we'll catch up to the remuda.'

Having seen the trouble, Dusty Fog turned his horse and headed to help Jeanie. The huge paint stallion he sat could run like a race-horse and he encouraged it to do so. On the other side of the wagon, Mark Counter galloped his great bloodbay stud-horse inwards. Converging on the remuda before it had time to scatter, the men brought it to a circling halt. Jeanie boiled up on her mare and the cowhands could see she was in a blazing temper.

'Did you see it?' she demanded. 'Did you see what that loco Scotch son-of-a-bitch pulled? He roped that mustang stallion!'

'The hell he did,' Dusty grinned. 'That Colin's got guts.'

'Guts!' Jeanie yelped. 'He's *loco*. Any kid'd know better than try roping a wild stallion when it came after the remuda. Damned if I know where he keeps his brains.'

'He's new to this game, Jeanie,' Dusty pointed out.

'And he's not likely to grow much older,' the girl snorted, 'happen that's the way he's going to act.'

'How'd you reckon Jeanie'd work out was she fresh arrived in Scotland, Dusty?' Mark inquired.

'Better than he's doing out here!' Jeanie replied hotly. 'You men're all alike, way you stand together.'

With that she swung her mare around and galloped towards the wagon. Colin rode out to meet her, after removing his rope from the dead stallion's neck.

'Thank you, Miss Jeanie——' he began.

'I'd've done it for anybody!' the girl snorted and went by him. Halting her horse alongside the wagon, she indicated the dead animal. 'Did you see it?'

'Sure,' Ma answered. 'Good hoss.'

'Real good,' Jeanie admitted.

'And Colin tried to catch it for you,' April went on. 'He's got guts enough to try, all he needs now is somebody to tell him what's right and wrong.'

A slight frown creased Jeanie's brow as she thought over the blonde's words. Maybe Colin had acted hastily; but, as April said, he had had the guts to try. If he did want to learn the mustanging business, it was only hospitable to help him. With Kenny out of the game, it fell on Jeanie to do the honours. Being Jeanie, she could not bring herself to display openly a change of mind.

'Maybe you're right,' she said and reined the mare around to ride after the remuda.

'You've got her thinking,' Ma grinned. 'Good thing that. It's time she eased off a mite on Colin. Like you'd know, you can ride a feller so long afore he rides away from you.'

'Are you match-making, Ma?' April asked with a smile.

'*Me*?' Ma gasped. 'As if I'd do a thing like that.'

Shaking his head sadly, Colin joined Dusty and Mark at the remuda. He felt, in view of Jeanie's attitude, that some explanation of his actions was necessary.

'I thought if I roped that horse Miss Jeanie would be pleased,' Colin told the Texans. 'No matter what I do, it seems to go wrong.'

'I'd worry about that,' Dusty replied. 'Only I figure you've got sense enough to learn from your mistakes. There's one thing you *can't* do and that's rope a wild stallion when it's acting like that one. It's got its mind dead set on one thing——'

'How'd you like it if you'd got a belly full of love, was set to go roosting with some pretty lil gal and somebody stopped you?' Mark interrupted. 'You'd be some riled, just like the stallion, likely.'

'Any time one comes at the remuda, it's hot after a mare,' Dusty went on. 'If you rope it, it'll turn on you and a bullet's all that'll stop it.'

'I didn't know,' Colin admitted. 'No stallion back home ever acted that way.'

'There's a big difference,' Dusty pointed out. 'These mustangs're wild animals, not somebody's strays. You interfere with near on any wild critter and it'll fight back.'

'Mind that next time, *amigo*?' Mark continued. 'And don't worry about this time. I'll go along with Dusty, you're smart enough to learn from your mistakes.'

At that moment Jeanie returned and the Texans left to resume their flanking guard. For a time the girl and Colin rode in silence. Then Jeanie's sense of fair play and humour took over and she chuckled. Luckily Colin realised that she was laughing with, not at, him and took it in a good spirit. By the time the party made camp for the night, Jeanie and Colin were on good terms. For the remainder of the day's journey she had answered his questions on things they saw, asked about conditions in Scotland and explained something of the work ahead.

The Kid rode into the camp area soon after dark. After caring for his wild-looking, magnificent white stallion—brought to Fort Sawyer along with the cattle—he announced that there was still no sign of pursuit. However he dismissed as unlikely Colin's suggestion that the Flores brothers had given up the idea of revenge.

'Could be they haven't got back to Fort Sawyer and learned we're gone yet,' the Kid guessed. 'One thing you can bet on, *amigo*. Once they know we've pulled out, they'll come looking and won't rest until they find you.'

In which the Kid proved a pretty fair judge of the situation, although wrong in a few small details.

Pushed hard by the cavalry patrol, the Flores gang had only that night returned to their hideout on Onion Creek. At about the same time as the Kid was giving his views on the situation, Matteo Flores walked into the fire-light's glow. Seated with his back to the wall of the small cave in which the remains of the gang hid, Tiburcio watched his brother clean the blade of the machete on his shirt sleeve.

'I caught Ramon sneaking off,' Matteo explained, sheathing the long-bladed weapon and looking at the five worried faces in the background. 'He's changed his mind about leaving.'

During the pursuit, two wounded men had been killed by the brothers. Since then there had been a growing restlessness among the rest of the gang. Several of the *bandidos* had managed to slip away. In fact only six remained with the brothers on their return to Onion Creek. It seemed that one of those chose to desert.

'Do any more of you want to go?' Tiburcio demanded, coming to his feet.

Only for a moment did the five *bandidos* hesitate with their reply. The brothers stood in a menacing attitude blocking the only way out of the cave. If there was any refusal to stay, its maker would die before he finished speaking. So a muted, sullen chorus of 'No' echoed hollowly from the men.

'That's better,' Tiburcio growled and sank on to his haunches again. 'What did you learn, Matteo?'

While his brother had come to Onion Creek and set up camp, Matteo went into the Mexican quarter of Fort Sawyer after information.

'Things are going badly for us,' Matteo answered. 'Hogan's been arrested by the Army and already the *peons* are saying we're finished.'

'We'll show them different when we get some more men,' Tiburcio promised.

'Only we won't get them unless we finish the bastard who killed our brothers and everybody who helped him,' Matteo pointed out.

'Is he still in town?'

'No. There's a wagon and horses behind the house, but not the ones we saw when we made the attack. They've gone.'

'Where to?'

'Mustanging. They took the man in the skirt and the blonde woman from the Black Bear with them.'

'Do you know where they went?' Tiburcio asked.

'I asked around,' Matteo answered. 'Nobody knows for sure. One girl said that the Schell family do most of their hunting along the Ronde River.'

'It's a start,' Tiburcio admitted. 'And we have to make one somewhere. We'll never get men to join us until we've killed the man in the skirt.'

'I want him,' Matteo snarled. 'The bastard shot my horse. I'll tear his guts out for that.'

'We'll have to find him first,' Tiburcio reminded. 'Let's sleep now and then start for the Ronde River country in the morning.'

At dawn, the gang set out. With their horses tired by the exertions of the past few days, Tiburcio knew that they could not hope to catch up to the Schell party as long as it kept moving. Trying to find and follow their tracks would also be too slow a process for him. That point was emphasised when another of the gang slipped away on the second night out of Onion Creek. Taking the warning, Tiburcio made the remaining four responsible for each other. He threatened to shoot any man who tried to desert and kill those left behind should one succeed in departing while he and Matteo slept. That prevented any further drain on their numbers. Going in a straight line for the lower reaches of the Ronde River, Tiburcio turned north and headed up-stream. In that way they ought to strike their quarry's tracks and be led to it.

Mile after mile fell behind them without a sign of the Schell party. Even Matteo's patience was wearing thin, while Tiburcio grew more morose and dangerous by the day. None of the gang showed any pleasure at the sight of a small, ruined, deserted village.

'We'll rest up here for a couple of days,' Tiburcio decided, looking at the two lines of tumble-down adobe shacks and the roofless wreck of a small church. 'There might be food and, anyway, the horses need the rest.'

Hiding their horses in the buildings, the men searched the village without finding anything edible or worth stealing. However they decided to stay on, for they could do some hunting to replenish their supply of meat. Towards nightfall, Matteo rose and picked up his Spencer rifle. Before he left the shack, he halted and peered through the window.

'A rider's coming,' he announced. 'One man. A *mestenero* from the look of him.'

Joining his brother, Tiburcio watched the man draw nearer. Big, thickset, he slouched in the saddle of a bay gelding. He rode with his head bent forward, the brim of the sombrero hiding his face. A serape hung across his shoulders, and he wore vaquero dress, with a revolver and knife at his belt. When the brothers stepped from the shack, the bay snorted. Jerking erect, the man started to grab at his gun but shot his hands into the air at the sight of the lined weapons. His surly, coarse face had a split, swollen lip and discoloured eye.

'I'm only a poor *m*——' he began.

'Who do you work for, *mestenero*?' Tiburcio interrupted.

'Nobody. I worked for the Schells until a son-of-a-whore wearing a skirt attacked me and ran me off.'

The words saved the man's life. Holstering his gun, Tiburcio gave a friendly chuckle and waved a hand towards the shack. 'Get down, *mestenero*. If you hate the man in the skirt, you are among friends.'

'Hate the bastard!' the man spat out. 'I'll tear his heart out and leave it for the buzzards.'

'Will you show us where their camp is?' Matteo demanded.

'I would,' the *mestenero* answered. 'Only I don't think there'll be any need.'

'Why not?' Tiburcio growled.

'I've been hid in a clump of mesquite most of the day with a large band of Indians making medicine not half a mile from me.'

'Indians?' Tiburcio breathed.

'Renegade Tejas mostly, maybe a hundred or more of them,' the *mestenero* elaborated. 'From the way they were headed when they rode off, they'll run right into the Schells' camp.'

Chapter Twelve

'Not much farther now,' Ma commented as the men gathered by the wagon for the noon meal on the seventh day out from Fort Sawyer. 'Our boys'll be camped down on the Owl Fork.'

'How about me going on ahead, Ma?' Jeanie suggested. 'I've got to tell Fernán that he's a father—again.'

'Go to it,' Ma smiled.

'Why'n't you come along, Colin?' the girl continued and eyed the three Texans at the fire with mock disgust. 'It's time these OD Connected yahoos did some work instead of just riding the rims.'

'Aye, that it is,' Colin agreed. 'How about it, Ma? I may be able to shoot another elk or something on the way.'

'Go to it,' Ma grinned. 'I reckon Dusty and Mark can handle the remuda.'

'Why don't you come and help us, April?' Mark inquired.

'You know what you can do with your horses,' the blonde snorted. 'I'm a big city gal and I just can't wait to get back to one.'

'Now that's a pity,' Ma chuckled. 'I was going to ask you to take on as cook for the outfit.'

Since leaving Fort Sawyer, April had handled the cooking to everybody's satisfaction. It had been several years since she prepared food in such primitive conditions, but she still remembered the best ways of doing so. However her reply to Ma's offer was blunt, to the point and reaffirmed her desire to return to her old way of life as soon as possible.

Letting Jeanie carry his Henry in the mare's saddleboot, Colin picked up his powerful double-barrelled rifle. Twice he had used the heavy weapon to bring down game, a buffalo bull and an elk falling to it. With the rifle resting on his knees, he rode away from the camp at the girl's side.

They saw no game on the journey and at last Jeanie reined in her horse on a rim. Halting at her side, Colin looked down at the *mestenero's* camp. It lay in the hollow of a U-shaped bend in a wide stream. At the bottom of the bend was a large corral with a number of horses in it. Beyond the corral stood a wagon, with a line of horses picketed along from it. Twenty-five or so Mexicans were gathered around a fire, squatting on their haunches and eating a meal served by a fat, jovial cook.

'Those horses are moving in a strange manner,' Colin commented. 'They look lame to me.'

'They're all right,' Jeanie replied. 'It's just that they've got *sarprimas* on. Ole Raoul's done good bringing this many in.'

Advancing down the slope, Jeanie felt surprised that none of the *mesteneros* came forward to greet her; not even Fernán, the fat, happy cook. He at least ought to be showing interest in her arrival. Followed by Colin, she rode down the slope and across the stream. While still wading through the water, Jeanie became aware of two details. Raoul, the segundo, was not present and the *sarprimas* on the horses had been secured in the wrong manner.

There were two ways of fixing a *sarprima*, a means of quietening down captured wild horses. The one insisted on by Trader Schell had been to girth the horse's body with a rawhide thong from which a strap coupled to the ankle of a front foot, in such a manner that it could use the foot when walking slowly but was brought down if it tried to run. Jeanie saw that the horses did not have that kind of *sarprima*. Instead the rope was passed around the animal's lower throat, between the forelegs and fastened to a hind fetlock, drawing the hoof from the ground. The girl knew this was a far more dangerous method than the first.

Nor did the flouting of her late father's orders end there. A block of wood hung from each horse's foretop, free to swing and bang its face when it moved.

Hot with anger, Jeanie dismounted and flung her reins to Colin. Then she stalked around the wagon and towards the fire. Fernán started to move forward, but the big, surly-looking man leaning against the side of the wagon scowled at him and he halted in his tracks.

'Where's Raoul?' Jeanie snapped, speaking Spanish with the ease of her native tongue.

'He had an accident,' the surly man answered. 'His horse fell and rolled on him. So I took over.'

Turning her eyes towards the speaker, Jeanie studied him coldly. Luis Cijar was a trouble-maker who her father had only hired because he had urgent need of an extra man. Of all the *mesteneros*, he had been the one she expected to make trouble on learning that Kenny was not with them. Moving from the wagon, he confronted the girl and grinned truculently at her. Jeanie stiffened slightly. To show weakness at that moment would mean a loss of control over the men.

'You just lost your chance,' she stated. 'Félix, you're segundo. Get the blocks off the horses' heads and fit the *sarprimas* properly.'

'Stay where you are!' Cijar snarled as the man Jeanie named started to rise. 'Who are you giving orders to, little girl?'

'I'm running things until my mother gets here!' Jeanie answered.

'Not Kenny?' Cijar inquired with a mocking leer.

'He'll be along!'

'Maybe he will—— Or maybe he got shot in Fort Sawyer. If he did, you've no man with you. We *mesteneros* won't take orders from a woman.'

'Does that go for all of you?' Jeanie asked.

'They'll do what I say,' Cijar growled. 'Now you get on your horse and go back to your mother. Tell her that we're working for ourselves.'

Instead of going, Jeanie turned her attention to the men around the fire. She saw worry, indecision, a little fear and concern on their faces. If there was only some way she could deal with Cijar, the men would follow her. Forgetting Colin's presence, Jeanie prepared to force a showdown with the surly trouble-maker.

'You're fired, Cijar!' she spat out. 'So get out of our ca——'

Before the words ended, Cijar caught her by the shoulder. His powerful fingers sank into her flesh, bringing a gasp of pain. 'I think maybe I'll teach you——'

Coming around the wagon, Colin took one quick look then moved forward. The men about the fire had been so interested in Jeanie's arrival, that they had overlooked the fact that she had a companion. After fastening the horses to the corral's top rail, Colin had followed the girl. While he did not understand the conversation, he could tell what Cijar meant by the man's attitude. Colin needed to know no more.

'Get your hands off her!' the Scot roared, catching Cijar by the left arm and swinging him around.

Bunching his left fist, Colin drove it into Cijar's face. The force of the blow split open the man's lip and he crashed into the wagon. Spitting out a curse, Cijar grabbed at his revolver and started to draw it. As the gun cleared leather, Colin bounded forward. Up lashed his left leg, the brogan smashing into the bottom of Cijar's hand and sending the gun spinning from it. With an almost animal-like screech, the *mestenero* grabbed for his knife with the left hand. Gliding in, Colin ripped a punch into Cijar's belly and knotted him over on to the other hand as it drove up. Hard knuckles slammed into the man's face and he lifted erect. Again Colin struck, crashing a blow to the side of Cijar's jaw. Pitching sideways, the man sprawled face down at Fernán's feet. Colin walked forward and jerked the knife from its sheath.

'*Hijo de yegua!*' the cook gasped, staring from Cijar to Colin. 'For a man who wears a skirt, you're plenty tough, *señor*.'

'This's Colin Farquharson,' Jeanie told the men after translating Fernán's compliment. 'Is he man enough to help us until Kenny can ride again?'

A mutter of assent rose from the men. Collecting a bucket of water from the side of the fire, Fernán emptied it over Cijar's head. For a moment the man continued to lie still, then his body writhed. Slowly he forced himself on to his hands and knees. After shaking his head, he turned over and sat on the grass. His eyes focussed on Colin and he spat out a curse. Grabbing at his right side, Cijar found an empty holster. From it, he grabbed for where his knife should be and found it too had gone.

'That's gone as well,' Fernán commented unnecessarily. 'And I wouldn't try to take it back. He's one tough *hombre* no matter how he dresses.'

Slowly Cijar dragged himself upright. Wiping the blood from his lip, he glared his hatred at the Scot. However, Cijar did not intend to take the matter further right then. One taste of Colin's hard fists had warned him of the other's potential in that line of fighting. Cijar decided he could wait for his revenge until a better chance presented itself.

'How did you know about Kenny?' Jeanie demanded, moving to Colin's side and looking at Cijar.

'He rode out two days after you left,' Fernán supplied when the *mestenero* did not answer. 'Came back on a half-dead horse three days ago. Told us that Kenny was killed and how he'd found Raoul dead.'

'What about Raoul?' the girl asked.

'Like Cijar said, his horse fell and rolled on him,' the cook answered. 'Cijar said you wouldn't be coming back, *señorita* and that he was boss. He's a bad *hombre* and we waited to see if he spoke the truth.'

'I'll get you for this, fat man!' Cijar spat out.

'You'll get out of our camp!' Jeanie corrected. 'All right, Félix, get the men to work. I want the *sar-primas* put right and the blocks taken off.'

'They're coming with me,' Cijar snarled. 'They won't take orders from a woman.'

'I don't go,' Fernán stated. 'And anybody else who does is a fool.'

'Which is it, *mesteneros*?' Jeanie went on. 'Go with him, or to the corral. Make your choice, *pronto*.'

For a moment none of the men moved. Then the short, leathery Félix rose and tossed his plate into the dish of water placed for that purpose.

'Let's get to work!' he ordered.

Man after man followed the new segundo's lead. Cijar glared at them, but to no avail. After being beaten by the Scot, he had lost his hold on the *mesteneros* and knew they would not obey him.

Watching the rage which played on Cijar's face, Jeanie knew that they could expect further trouble from him should he remain in the vicinity. However she figured that she could move him on.

'You know *Cabrito*?' she asked.

'Sí,' Cijar answered sullenly; no great surprise, for the Ysabel Kid's fame covered the border country.

'He's coming with my mother. When he gets here, I'm going to ask him to ride out to the place where Raoul died and see what can be learned. Maybe he'll want to see you when he gets back.'

Slowly concern wiped the anger from Cijar's face and Jeanie knew her point had been taken. Everybody along the bloody border had heard of *Cabrito's* almost uncanny ability to read sign. Worry worked on Cijar's face. Maybe the Kid would find something Cijar's presence had caused the other *mesteneros* to miss. If so, the man had no wish to be interviewed on the subject; especially by the black-dressed *Tejano* called *Cabrito*.

'I'm going now,' Cijar muttered. 'You give me my gun and knife?'

'Aye,' Colin agreed when Jeanie explained the request. 'Only I'll take the percussion caps off the revolver first.'

While that was being done, Cijar gathered his belongings and collected his horse. On the return of his weapons, he swung into the saddle and rode away from the camp. Colin stood watch, holding the double-barrelled rifle—which he had left leaning on the rear of the wagon when dealing with Cijar—until the man passed out of sight. Then the young Scot joined the girl as she supervised the improvements to the horse's conditions.

By the time the wagon arrived, Jeanie had everything to her satisfaction. She told her mother and the Texans of Raoul's death and Cijar's behaviour.

'Get one of the *mesteneros* to show you where it happened, Lon,' Dusty ordered. 'Way that feller took off could mean he knows how the hoss happened to fall.'

'What'll I do happen it wasn't an accident?' asked the Kid.

'Bring Cijar back here,' Dusty replied. 'Likely we'll think of something.'

'You choosey how he comes back?' drawled the Kid.

'If he killed Raoul, bring him in any way you have to,' Dusty answered and Ma Schell nodded her approval.

Going out to the place where the segundo had died, the Kid made a thorough examination of the area. He failed to find anything to say how the horse came to fall, but decided that Dusty would want definite evidence before having Cijar fetched in. Despite all his sterling qualities, Dusty possessed what the Kid considered too high a regard for the sanctity of human life. So the Kid returned to the camp and reported his findings. After some discussion, it was decided to let Cijar go and count it as good riddance to a worthless trouble-causer.

That night the whole party held a celebration in honour of the remount contract and the birth of Fernán's eighth child. Dawn found them making preparations for beginning the hunts. During a council of war held around the breakfast fire, Colin learned something of the way the hunts would be run. To his surprise, he found that they would not attempt to break any of the horses captured. Instead they were to let the mustangs settle down, then introduce them to a bunch of gentle mares—which had been range-grazing away from the camp on Colin's arrival—and rely on herd instinct to hold them all together. Stallions would be gelded when captured, to prevent them fighting among themselves or trying to scatter with the mares.

The thirty or so horses already captured had been taken in *corrals de espiar*, spy or night pens. Simple to construct, being no more than a pole corral around a known watering place, they were left with the gates open. A hidden man kept watch until the mustangs entered to drink, then closed the entrance. However there had been a couple of days with heavy rain which made *corrals de espiar* practically useless. The mustangs could find water easily and no longer needed to rely upon the regular, always productive holes.

From then on, the mustangers would rely on *corridas*, driving the *mestenas*, into large, stoutly-made wing corrals. After discussing the situation with Félix and the *mesteneros*, Jeanie decided that they would make their first *corrida* using a corral about a mile from their present camp. With a calm efficiency that delighted Colin, the girl took command and gave her orders. Sending the Kid and Félix out to scout the *mestenas* and select the best route to make the *corrida*, she led the rest of the men to see what repairs needed making to the corral.

Colin expected to see an ordinary circular pole

corral, with triple bars running horizontally between upright supports. Instead he found himself confronted with a large pallisade of logs. Looking down the steep side of a canyon, he could see that one wing extended to each side of its lower end and that the wall of the corral formed a spiral rather than a circle.

'It's a *caracol* pen,' Jeanie explained. 'That means "snail". Once the hosses get inside, they can't double back.'

'Suppose they won't come down this valley?' Colin inquired.

'We'll tend to that,' the girl promised. 'Let me go see what the fence wants doing to it first though. It's no use making the *corrida* and then have the hosses break through the side of the corral.'

'I see that,' Colin admitted.

'With luck, there'll be two to three hundred head inside,' Jeanie went on. 'The corral has to be strong. We haven't used this one for three years, it'll likely need plenty of fixing.'

Which comment showed that the girl possessed good judgement. In the course of her examination, Jeanie discovered and pointed out a number of faults which needed attention before a *corrida* could be brought to a successful conclusion.

'That gate needs clearing so it'll close,' she announced. 'See to the hinges while you're at it.'

'I'll tend to it, Jeanie,' Mark offered and the girl nodded her agreement.

'These posts want replacing,' Jeanie went on, indicating some of the wall's supports after assigning men to help Mark. 'Will you tend to it, Dusty?'

'You're the boss,' Dusty answered.

'Lend him a hand, Colin,' the girl ordered. 'Then we'll start re-roping the uprights, that raw-hide don't look any too strong.'

Work on the corral continued through the day and next morning Colin found himself handed a shovel. Other of the men collected picks and shovels from the family wagon and Jeanie took them on to the open range by the outer mouth of the canyon. While riding there, the girl explained what had to be done next.

'You boys have to clear a yard-wide strip of earth for a distance of half a mile on each side of the canyon, starting from its mouth. I mean clear it, grass, bushes, everything. Widen the other end so you're maybe half a mile apart when you've done.'

'And then put up a fence?' Colin asked.

'Nope. Just the furrows,' Jeanie replied. 'The mustangs'd see a fence as we haze them in. They'll not see the furrows until they're right on them.'

'Won't they just run across?'

'They never have yet. Don't ask me why, but they'll not try to cross the black strip of open ground.'

Having decided that Jeanie knew what she was doing, Colin set to work without further debate. Although he had done little digging, he threw himself into the task whole-heartedly and drew grins of admiration from his work-party. Already the *mesteneros* had grown accustomed to his kilt and his handling of Cijar prevented any adverse comments on it. By night fall they had one strip completed and the other half cut. Nothing could have given the young Scot greater pleasure than when Jeanie told him he had done real well.

By noon the following day the furrows had been completed and the *caracol* made ready to take the *mestenas* at the end of the *corrida*. Félix and the Kid had scouted out the surrounding ranges and reported that there were a number of herds of varying size, including three bands of young stallions that would form a fine nucleus for the remount contract.

'You boys can rest up today,' Jeanie told the men around the fire. 'Cull out and de-pride the stallions in the corral there. Tomorrow's Sunday. Monday, we'll start the *corrida*.'

'What're you going to do, Jeanie?' Mark grinned. 'Sit on your butt and watch the help working like most bosses——'Cepting you, that is, Dusty.'

'Is that loyalty or just scared he'll remember it

when you're back on the ranch?' April asked from where she was helping to prepare the evening meal.

'Both,' Mark admitted. 'How about it, Jeanie-gal?'

'I'm going to see how that lil dun of mine takes to me on the saddle,' the girl replied.

On the day of her arrival, Jeanie had selected a horse from those captured in her absence. It was a small but shapely dun stallion with lines hinting at speed and stamina. Having it cut from the others and penned alone, she began the process of winning its trust. So far she had done no more than let it grow accustomed to the feel of the saddle. With the afternoon free, she hoped to carry the training a stage farther by riding it.

The hope did not materialise. Having left that morning with the intention of making a long circle around the camp, looking for signs of the Flores gang, the Kid returned hurriedly just as Jeanie planned to visit the dun. Swinging from his horse, the Kid went straight up to Dusty.

'There's a bunch of Injuns coming, Dusty. Seventy or so, Tejas mostly.'

'They're horse-hunting, likely,' Dusty replied, for the Tejas tribe had long been noted for its friendship with the white man.

'I don't reckon so,' contradicted the Kid. 'There's a few Kaddo and Waco bucks along with 'em.'

'Renegades then,' Mark stated. 'No friendly Tejas'd ride with Kaddo and Wacos along.'

'They know we're around, Lon?' Dusty asked.

'Saw your smoke, I'd say,' answered the Kid. 'What're you fixing to do?'

At such a time Jeanie did not offer to give orders. Came to gun-trouble, she rated yearling stock compared with the small, soft-spoken Texan. All eyes went to Dusty as those *mesteneros* who spoke English told the others what had been said. Dusty did not reply for a moment, but his eyes went to the Winchester in the Kid's hand. An idea took form and Dusty gave his orders for trying it out.

'Colin, Mark, get your rifles and saddle your horses. Ma, have everything made ready for a fight if it comes. Can you count on your men?'

'Like on you,' Ma replied.

'I'll take the double and leave Ma the Henry,' Colin suggested.

'No!' Dusty answered. 'Leave the double. You'll need that Henry and a full box of shells.'

Chapter Thirteen

Riding with the Texans and listening to Dusty's plan, Colin lost some of his misgivings at bringing his Henry when there was only one magazine rifle at the camp. When Dusty had finished the explanation, Colin waited to hear the other two cowhands' views.

'It could work,' Mark decided. 'They'll most of them never've seen a repeater afore.'

'Them Tejas ain't real fighting Injuns,' the Kid went on. 'And any Kaddo or Waco who'd ride with 'em's not likely to be any great shucks as a brave-heart. I'll go along with you, Dusty. Less'n you want to play it safe by laying for 'em and giving 'em a real notion of what a Henry'll do.'

'Now ain't that just what you'd expect from a danged *Tshaoh*?' Mark snorted. 'There's no wonder the other tribes called you *Nemenuh** the Enemy People.'

'He's not fit company for hard-working, church-going folks,' Dusty replied.

'Which I ain't with none of, anyways,' the Kid declared. 'Play it your fool way then. Only when they've killed 'n' scalped us, I'll come up and say, "I told you so." Not that we're likely to wind up at the same place.'

'If we do,' grinned Mark. 'I'll ask to go the other way.'

After which they became serious. Riding south for

**Tshaoh, Nemenuh:* Two names for the Comanche nation.

over a mile, they topped a rim and came face to face with the Indians. About a hundred yards separated the two parties, but the braves were at the foot of the slope. Looking down, Colin felt a touch disappointed. Going by paintings he had seen, he expected the Indians to be tall, impressive men dressed in decorative buckskins and sporting trailing feather war bonnets. Instead the men below were squatly built, clad in a mixture of filthy buckskins and cast-off white men's garments. Only a few carried muzzle-loading rifles, the rest being armed with lances or bow and arrows. Reining in their horses, they showed surprise and broke into a jabber of talk at the sight of the four riders.

'Give me just two lil *Pehnane tuivitsi** and I'll run the whole stinking boiling of 'em back where they come from,' sniffed the Kid.

'Go talk to them a mite,' Dusty ordered.

Advancing a short way down the slope, the Kid raised his right hand in a peace sign. Then he spoke in the Tejas language. Riding forward, a stocky man, with a rifle on the crook of his arm and eagle feather stuck into the band of a battered Burnside campaign hat, replied. He spoke at length, accompanied by grunts from the other braves.

'Wanted to know what we're doing here, Dusty,' the Kid announced without turning his back on the Indians. 'I told him. So he allows that this's Tejas country and we've go to pay him afore we can hunt here.'

'How much does he want?' Colin inquired.

'Half of all the hosses we catch. Keg of gunpowder, lead for bullets, caps, knives, presents for his wives for starters,' the Kid replied. 'Likely he'd think out a few more, given time.'

'Is this their land, Dusty?' Colin asked.

'Naw, and never was,' scoffed the Kid. 'What do I tell him, Dusty?'

'To go to hell and roast there,' the small Texan an-

**Tuivitsi:* Young, inexperienced brave.

swered. Then, hearing a low hiss from the young Scot, went on, 'It's the only way, Colin. Give in to their kind and they'll come back for more. When you get tired of giving, or they don't want you any more, they'll jump you. So we don't start giving.'

The Kid had been addressing the Indians while Dusty made his point to Colin. Still not taking his eyes from the men below, the dark youngster spoke over his shoulder.

'He says he's got fifteen hands of brave-hearts. Stinking liar—there's not more'n half that many. Allows they'll stop us hunting and take what they want.'

'Tell him we'll have something to say about that,' Dusty commanded. 'Do like I said, Colin, unless they keep coming up. If they do, shoot to kill.'

When the Kid repeated Dusty's warning, the Indians milled around and talked among themselves. Then they backed their horses away from the foot of the slope and formed into a line.

'Ready?' Dusty asked, slanting the muzzle of his carbine upwards and pressing its trigger.

On the heels of the shot, Mark, the Kid and Colin also sent a bullet into the air. Their actions appeared to surprise the Indians. However, even a bunch of Tejas renegades could understand the chance the white-eye brother was throwing their way. For some reason each of the four white men had emptied his rifle. That was their misfortune, a gift from the Great Spirit no right-thinking brave could pass up. So the warriors started their horses moving forward.

Then they saw the white men swing the rifles into line but the sight caused them no concern—at first. Suddenly, despite the fact that no ramrod or powder flask had been used, the rifles spat again; and again and again. Lead screamed down the slope as the Texans and Colin made use of the inventive genius of Mr. B. Tyler Henry. Ricochets wailed in the horses' faces and bullets fanned by their riders. The effects of the rapid fire was all Dusty hoped for. Startled horses reared, men reined their mounts into turns or sliding stops. None of the braves had seen a repeating rifle, few of which had reached Texas. Even the Union Army still equipped its men with single-shots, so the Indians had yet to learn the devastating effect of lever-action mechanisms and large capacity magazines.

'Spirit guns!' a brave screeched.

Which just about summed up the feelings of the rest of the band. The hint of supernatural intervention proved the final straw to break the back of the attack. Whirling their horses around, the Indians fled across the range. Dusty and his companions lowered their smoking rifles and watched the departure.

'Whooee!' whooped the Kid. 'Grandpappy Long Walker'll laugh fit to bust a gut when I tell him about this.'

'Will they be back?' Colin inquired, feeling slightly cheated at the lack of spirit shown by the braves.

'Naw!' scoffed the Kid. 'If they'd been Comanches——'

'I wouldn't've tried it,' Dusty interrupted. 'You'd maybe best trail along after them, Lon. See them on their way, then make a circle and cut for sign of the Flores bunch.'

'Yo!' answered the Kid. 'How soon do you want me back?'

'Take all the time you want,' Dusty told him. 'Only try to be back by Monday to start work.'

'I just knowed you'd say that,' the Kid grinned.

Riding back over the rim with the other three, the Kid halted his horse on the other side. They left him waiting to make a start at his work and continued on their way to the camp. Looking around as he approached the wagon, Dusty found that Ma had organised its defence very well. The *mesteneros* and women left the places from which they would have made their fight as the trio came up.

'You pulled it off, huh?' Ma asked, cradling the Henry on her arm.

'Looks that way,' Dusty replied. 'I sent Lon to see

them on their way. We didn't kill any of them, so they'll likely not be back.'

'Let's hope they don't come back,' Jeanie remarked, putting the Sharps carbine into the wagon. 'We can do without Injun fuss.'

Within a short time work around the camp was resumed. Assisted by the Texans, Jeanie gave her dun its first taste of being ridden. To lessen the chances of injury to herself and the horse, she had it led belly-deep into the stream before mounting. Doing so prevented the horse from bucking wildly, although it managed to dump her into the water once. Before nightfall it would allow the girl to sit on its back while in the stream. However Jeanie knew it would be a different tale when she first tried riding on dry land.

Sunday passed quietly and without the Kid returning. His absence caused the others no concern. All his early life had been spent preparing for such missions and he could be relied upon to stalk the Tejas unseen by any of them. Jeanie gave her dun another session in the water, then tried on land. After a session of bucking, the horse started to run. Followed by Colin, Jeanie allowed the dun to run itself out and returned to the camp with it in a subdued condition. Although she had won another stage for control, her every instinct warned that the fight was not yet over.

In the afternoon Jeanie accompanied Colin and Dusty on a hunting trip from which they returned with two whitetail deer. After supper, Colin unloaded his trunk and took out the cleaning kit for the big double rifle.

'What are these, *señor*?' Fernán asked, indicating the bagpipes which Colin had left on top of the trunk.

'Why not play a tune on them and show him?' April suggested with a grin.

'Sure,' Ma went on, 'I've seed 'em afore and wondered what kind of music they made.'

'I warn you the pipes are an acquired taste,' Colin

smiled, rising to comply with the request. 'But to a Scot, there's no music in the world like them.'

Watching Colin tuck the tartan-covered bag under his left arm, erect the four beribboned pipes and place the chanter to his lips, Jeanie decided that she would acquire the required taste if it pleased him. Sucking in a deep breath, Colin started to blow. After a low murmur, the pipes began to wail in their eerie, dirge-like yet beautiful manner. Startled expressions broke from the *mesteneros* and Ma stared at the young Scot as he strode up and down before the fire.

'Damned if I don't try to da——' April began.

And at that moment the horses gave notice that they had not acquired a taste for Highland music. Snorting and rearing, the mounts on the picket-line fought at the securing rope. In the larger pen, the mustangs heard and panicked. Two went down, then a third as they tried to move faster than the *sarprimas* allowed.

'Cut it out, Colin!' Dusty yelled, bounding to his feet. 'Get to the picket-line some of you. Down to the night-pen, Félix.'

'My dun!' Jeanie shouted, snatching up her rope and darting off into the darkness.

Pandemonium reigned briefly around the fire but Dusty's orders sent men scurrying to obey. Tossing his pipes on to the trunk, Colin scooped up his own rope and leapt after Jeanie. Once clear of the fire, his eyes quickly grew accustomed to the darkness. Running at his best speed, he went by the girl. Ahead he could see the dun stallion racing around the corral. Then it headed for the fence in his direction, gathering itself for a jump. Even as the horse took off, Colin shook free the loop of his rope. Much of his spare time, all that could be given when not learning the art of quick-draw, had gone to practicing with the lariat. For all that, he felt nervous as the dun sailed over the corral rails towards him. If Jeanie lost the horse, she would hold him responsible and go back to her old way of treating him. Muttering a silent prayer, he sent the loop flying out. With elation he saw that he had thrown true—and remembered the last occasion that he roped a stallion. Then he had been on a horse. Now he was a-foot and the situation would be even more dangerous.

Plunging by Colin, the stallion ran on. Grimly the Scot set his teeth and dug in his heels as he prepared to fight against the jolting pull that must come. Just before it happened, Jeanie arrived and grabbed the rope ahead of him.

'Heave back as hard as you can!' the girl yelled.

Obediently Colin threw all his weight to the rear. Nine hundred pounds of running horse rushed towards the end of the rope. However the lariat snapped tight about its neck and struck its flank, giving a warning. Having already learned the futility of fighting against a choking noose, the dun did not try. Showing the agility which had so attracted Jeanie when she first saw it, the horse came around on its hind legs.

With a deft flick, Jeanie sent the loose rope curling out to encircle the dun's sky-pawing forelegs. A jerk drew them together and when the horse landed it crashed on to its side.

'Keep him down, Colin!' Jeanie ordered, darting to snatch up her own lariat. 'I'll get my rope on him and we can take him back.'

Winded by the fall, the dun made no further fight on being released. After they had led it into the corral, Colin stood and looked around. In the night-pen Dusty and Mark examined the horses with the aid of a lantern from the wagon. Félix rode up to say that, although disturbed, the lead-mares still held together. Clearly the picket-line had held, but Ma and one of the men were checking on the state of the holding stakes.

'I'm sorry, Jeanie,' Colin said at the girl came to his side.

'It's our fault more than you'n,' the girl replied. 'We ought to've known how easy the horses spook. How'd you fix to stop the dun?'

'I never gave it a thought,' Colin admitted.

'Even after what happened last time?'

'It was *your* horse, lass. I didn't mean to let it go.'

'You crazy Scotch yahoo!' Jeanie breathed, turning to face him. 'You risked your neck for me.'

Next moment she was in his arms and their lips met. After a moment they separated and stood looking at each other.

'I—I'm sorry,' Colin whispered.

'Damned if I am,' Jeanie replied. 'I liked it—— Come on, let's get back and see if there's anything we can do.'

'It'd be best,' Colin agreed. 'Will the dun be all right in there?'

'I reckon so. After the way he lit down, he'll not feel like jumping again for a spell.'

On their return to the fire, Jeanie and Colin found the others coming back. Before any of them could speak, the girl launched into a defence for Colin.

'It wasn't his fault,' she announced.

'Nobody says it was,' Ma replied. 'Only I'd's soon we didn't have any more bagpipe music 'round the camp.'

'I warned you the pipes are an acquired taste,' Colin pointed out. 'Did any of the horses hurt themselves?'

'Few bruises, some with the wind knocked out of them is all,' Dusty replied. 'We'd best take a longer look in the morning through.'

'Sure,' Ma agreed.

Once more the group gathered about the fire and the conversation welled up. Fernán returned Colin's bagpipes, discarded in the rush to prevent the dun escaping, and Dusty watched the Scot put them back into the trunk.

'Ma,' the small Texan said. 'What's the hardest part of a *corrida*?'

'Trader allus reckoned getting the hosses going the way you want 'em to and not busting back away from the *caracol*.'

'There're a couple of *mestenas* up this way that must have bust out of a corral,' Jeanie went on.

'Now they'll not drive. As soon as you try, they turn and run back towards you. Once that happens, more of 'em go along. Why, Dusty?'

'It's just a fool notion,' Dusty replied. 'But I think I know how we can make them go the way we want.'

'How?' Jeanie asked.

'With those bagpipes,' Dusty explained. 'If Colin gets at the back of the range we're fixing to drive and rides towards the *caracol* playing 'em, the mustangs will head away from him.'

'They might at that,' Jeanie admitted and explained the scheme to Félix who grinned broadly and answered. Also smiling, the girl translated for Colin's benefit. 'Félix's for it. He reckons that he near on headed for the high country his-self when you cut loose with 'em, Colin boy.'

'Tell him he's no taste for good music, lass,' Colin suggested.

'Will you do it for us, Colin?' Ma asked.

'That I will, Ma,' the Scot agreed. 'We may have to plug my horse's ears though. He might not have a taste for good music either.'

Having adopted Dusty's scheme, Ma and the others discussed it for a time and decided how it could best be carried out. With the arrangements made, they turned in for the night. Double guards kept watch in case the Tejas returned, but dawn came without the Indians making an appearance.

There would be a delay before setting out to make the *corrida*, while the mustangs in the night-pen received a more thorough examination than had been possible by lantern light. So Jeanie decided to give the dun a work-out. On her arrival at the corral, she found the horse acting in a subdued manner and had little difficulty in saddling it. Nor did it protest as she led it to the stream, then mounted in the water. After a short time, she steered the dun ashore. It stood for a moment and she prepared to ride out in a spate of bucking. However the expected protest did not come, so she gently started the dun moving and rode it to where the men were gathered.

'How's this?' Jeanie asked, looking to where Colin was slinging the bagpipes over his shoulder by their carrying strap.

'You've done real we——' the Scot began.

Pride on his face, Fernán moved forward to take a better look at the girl. In doing so, he knocked a pile of tin plates from the bench formed by the tail-gate of the wagon. They landed on the hard earth with an unholy clatter. Instantly the dun blew out a snort, bounded into the air almost unseating its rider and took off on the run.

Although taken by surprise, Jeanie did not panic. She had been riding almost since the day she learned to walk and acted automatically. Clamping hold of the saddle with her legs, she caught her balance and started to pull on the reins to regain control. Immediately she knew that she was in trouble. During the jolt from landing on the startled bound, the dun had managed to get the bit between its teeth. Which meant that she could not hope to control it by the reins.

'Damn this fool stupid horse!' she muttered. 'All right, blast you, run 'til you're ready to stop. I can take it as long as you can—and you'll still have to carry me back.'

With that she composed herself for what she knew would be a long, fast ride and gave her full attention to staying on the racing dun's back.

At the sight of the dun taking off, the *mesteneros* hooted with laughter. All of them at one time or another had been carried off in a similar manner and regarded it as a part of their work. Knowing Jeanie's ability as a horsewoman, they felt no anxiety for her safety.

Not so Colin. Seeing one of the men had led up his bay to be saddled, he raced towards it. Going aside its bare back, he snatched the hackamore from the man's hand. With a wild yell, the Scot started the horse running in pursuit of the girl he loved.

'Want for us to go after them, Ma?' Mark inquired.

'Naw,' she answered. 'They'll do all right without us. Best give them half an hour and if they're not back by then start the *corrida* without them.'

'Jeanie'll be pot-boiling mad if we do,' Dusty pointed out. 'She wants for Colin to have his chance to make good.'

'You're right about that,' Ma admitted. 'It's be best to wait for them.'

Time went by without Jeanie and Colin reappearing. None of the others were worried for they knew a spooked horse so recently caught would run a considerable distance before coming to a halt. Then it would need to cool out and rest up before making the return journey. Following the Texas tradition, Colin strapped on his gunbelt while dressing. So he carried the loaded Dragoon Colt and dirk as a means of defence. Dusty considered the Scot well able to handle the revolver should the need arise.

'Lon's coming!' Mark snapped.

Watching the black dressed youngster gallop towards them, Dusty knew there was trouble in the air. Sweat lathered the stallion's flanks and it showed signs of long, fast travel. Mark sprang forward to take the reins as the Kid dismounted and began to walk the horse until it cooled down.

'Those damned Tejas!' the Kid gasped as April ran forward carrying a mug of water. 'They've met up with the Flores bunch and the whole boiling of 'em're headed this way.'

Once again Dusty took charge. 'Get the mares brought in, Félix!' he barked. 'Mark, take some men and have the *sarprimas* off the mustangs. Manuel, take the horses from the picket line into the corral. Then grab your rifles ready for a fight. Do you want me to send Lon and some of the boys after Jeanie and Colin, Ma?'

For a moment the woman hesitated, then she shook her head. 'We'll need every gun right here,' she decided. 'When they hear the shooting, they'll guess what's happened and stay clear until it's safe to come in.'

Chapter Fourteen

Never had Colin ridden as he did while urging his mount after Jeanie's speeding bay. Paying no attention to his surroundings, he concentrated on keeping the girl in sight. He knew that he could not hope to overhaul the dun, which carried a lighter load—even with its saddle—than the bay. Nor did the distance increase greatly, for the horse he rode was a running fool.

All in all Jeanie was enjoying the ride. Before they had gone far, she knew that the dun was not running blind. It avoided such obstacles as lumps of rock or clumps of mesquite, showing no inclination to try crashing into either. With cat-footed ease, it slid down slopes and rocketed up others as if its mother had been part big-horn sheep. Although it made for a sizeable *bosque*, she felt no anxiety. Knowing there was no way to hold it, she gave her full attention to evading branches. She felt something catch her right sleeve, but the material tore before she could be dragged out of the saddle.

Following the girl, Colin marvelled at her riding skill. He could tell that the horse had the bit between its teeth and felt admiration at the way in which his Jeanie stayed with it. Ahead of the dun lay a stream and it sailed across like a whitetail deer bounding over a log. Setting his teeth, Colin guided the bay towards the water. Gathering itself, it leapt and lit down on the other shore to resume the pursuit through the trees.

Through the *bosque* they went, then across the rolling, open country. A small *mestena* broke out of a draw and ran ahead of the dun. At the sight of its own kind, the horse gave chase. For their part, the mustangs had seen the girl on the dun's back and Colin coming up in the rear. So they fled at their best speed, hazed on and guided by their stallion.

Over four miles had falled behind Jeanie and Colin since leaving the camp. At last the girl could feel her horse tiring. Yet it kept up its attempts to catch up with the *mestena*. Driven by the fear of their human pursuers, the mustangs swung into the mouth of a canyon. Naturally the dun followed and Colin brought up the rear.

Thundering along the floor of the canyon, the mustangs found it came to a blind end. On the right, the slope rose too steeply to be climbed and at the left the side rose almost vertically as did the end. So the horses whirled about and rushed back towards the entrance. Jeanie's dun saw them coming and also tried to go around. Charging through its mares, the herd stallion smashed into the dun's rump as it went by. Knocked staggering, the dun screamed and started to go down.

With the skill of years behind her, Jeanie quit the saddle of her falling mount. Lighting down on the run, she saw horses flashing by and dived behind a rock. Crouched in its shelter, she turned to see Colin sliding off the bare back of his rearing, spooked bay. On landing, the Scot threw himself clear of the bay's churning legs. Much as he wanted to try to catch the horse, he saw there would be no chance. The mustangs thundered towards him and would run him down before he could do so. There was only once chance for Colin for he could see no rock large enough to offer him shelter. Diving, he flattened himself belly down on the ground and relied upon the wild horses' aversion to trampling on strange objects to save him. The gamble paid off. Most of the mustangs swerved around him, but two hurdled his body without touching him and he rose unharmed as the *mestena* streamed out of the canyon accompanied by his bay.

Ignoring his lost horse, Colin rose and turned towards Jeanie. The girl ran forward and threw herself into his arms.

'Are you all right, Jeanie lass?' he asked gently after kissing her.

'Sure,' she replied. 'I thought they'd tromp you flat——'

'You saved me.'

'How?'

'By telling me how horses wouldn't cross a furrow. I figured that they might not trample me if I lay still.'

They stood in the embrace for a moment, then a squeal of pain from the dun brought their attention its way. One look told them all they needed to know. Although the horse tried to rise, its near fore-leg would not support its weight.

'Broken!' Colin said, releasing the girl and making a closer examination of the dun's injury.

'Damn it to hell!' Jeanie cursed bitterly. 'Let me have your gun, Colin.'

'I'll do it,' he told her. 'Go wait by the end of the canyon.'

If any other man had made the suggestion, Jeanie would have felt indignant and refused. In Colin's case, she raised no objections. Helping him to remove her saddle, she dragged it aside and then walked back towards the canyon's mouth. Much as the Scot hated the thought, he knew what must be done. Drawing and cocking the Dragoon, he took aim at the centre of the horse's head. Jeanie did not turn as the revolver boomed. Walking slowly on, she heard Colin approaching. Placing his arm across her shoulders, he squeezed her gently.

'It was a good hoss,' Jeanie said.

'We'll catch more of them,' Colin promised, then a disturbing thought struck him and he put it as lightly as he could. 'If we can find our way back to the camp, that it.'

'Why shouldn't we?' Jeanie asked in surprise.

'I hadn't time to watch where we were going,' Colin confessed. 'We could be anywhere for all I know.'

If she had heard Colin admit such a thing earlier in their acquaintance, Jeanie would have regarded it as a further example of his general incompetence. To a girl born and raised on the great open range country of Texas, finding one's way from place to place came naturally. Like most children of the plains, Jeanie had developed an inborn ability to remember which direction she had travelled without conscious need to watch the route taken. Added to that, she knew the area around the Ronde River very well and so experienced none of the Scot's concern.

'I'll show you where the camp is as soon as we're out of here,' she told him.

So they walked on, Colin with his right arm still around Jeanie's shoulders and her saddle in his left hand. He felt complete confidence in the girl's ability to direct them to the camp. More than that, he expected that Ma and Dusty would have sent riders after them. If so, they would be saved the long walk back.

With that thought in mind, Colin started to look around him as they emerged from the canyon. As his head swung towards the right, he saw something which appeared to confirm his belief that a search party was on its way.

'Look, Jeanie,' he said, taking his arm from the girl and pointing. 'We won't have to walk far.'

Following the direction Colin indicated, Jeanie saw four riders emerge slowly from the distant *bosque*. They were too far away for her to even guess at their identity, but she felt worried by their presence. Then two flickers of reflected sunlight sparkled from them.

'Get back into the canyon!' she hissed.

Retreating hurriedly in response to the urgency in the girl's voice, Colin lowered the saddle to the ground. He rejoined her at the mouth, noticing how she peered cautiously around the edge of the wall.

'What's wrong, lass?' he whispered. 'They're some of your *mesteneros*—aren't they?'

'I don't reckon so. Ma wouldn't send four men out after us and I'm near on sure that flickering was from the heads of warlances.'

'Indians?'

'Yeah!'

Looking out across the range, Colin studied the four men. Like Jeanie, he could tell nothing about them. He was willing to accept her judgement and gave his attention to the immediate future.

'What are they after, lass?'

'Us. That was about where we left the *bosque*. Likely they're on our trail.'

'That's bad,' Colin said, right hand brushing the grips of the Dragoon.

'Real bad,' Jeanie agreed. 'If we go out, they'll see us and if we stay put, they'll have us boxed in.'

'Aye,' agreed Colin. 'Even if we slipped out, they'd find our tracks and follow. They can move faster than we can on foot. There's only four of them——'

'Scouts ahead of the main bunch, likely,' Jeanie pointed out. 'We've only got five bullets in the gun.'

'I've my dirk and *sgian-dubh*,' Colin went on, pointing to the weapon on his belt and small knife in his stocking. 'But fighting isn't the answer.'

'There's no place to hide,' Jeanie warned.

'Not down here,' Colin agreed. 'But there will be up on top.'

'We could maybe go up that side,' Jeanie said doubtfully, looking at the right-hand slope.

'Aye. But we're going up *this* side,' Colin told her.

For a moment the girl stared at the wall, then she gulped and turned her eyes to Colin's face. '*This* side?'

'They'll not expect it, lass. Come on, we've little enough time to do it.'

'How about my saddle?'

'We'll have to leave it, but we'll need your rope. Take it and fasten one end around you while I put your saddle so it'll lead them astray.'

Taking the rope from her saddlehorn, Jeanie, knotted its end about her waist. Then she followed Colin as he carried the saddle to conceal it among some rocks at the foot of the slope. With that done, he crossed to the other side and walked along studying the wall. Back in Scotland, climbing had been his hobby since a boy. So he brought to bear all his knowledge on the business of selecting a spot up which Jeanie might climb with his assistance. As last he made his choice. A point sufficiently far down the canyon for them to be hidden from the approaching men and offering a variety of foot or hand holds.

'Come up after me, Jeanie,' he told her, knotting the rope's other end around him. 'Keep the rope hanging loose, but not dangling too much. And if you get into trouble, stop and tell me straight away.'

'S—Sure,' Jeanie gulped.

Scooping her into his arms, Colin planted a kiss on her lips. He could feel her body stiffen and knew that he could rely on her to do as he said. Turning, he began to climb up the wall. Jeanie stood below him, looking upwards and trying to remember the places where he rested his weight or which he used to haul himself higher. Then her gaze turned to the wall. From the ground, its eighty or so foot of height seemed far greater. Always something of a tomboy, Jeanie had climbed slopes and trees as a youngster; but she had never attempted such an ascent. Only her faith in Colin gave her the courage to make the try.

Slowly, feeling her way with groping fingers and toes, the girl pulled herself upward. At first the climb was comparatively easy. Then the strain began to tell on her wiry little body. Sweat soaked her, but she continued to drag herself higher. One foot slipped from its place, scrabbled and found another crack into which it dug. For a moment she hung there, gasping and shuddering. Only by exerting all her will power did she manage to raise the lower foot in search of the next support.

'C—Colin!' she gasped.

'Keep coming, lassie,' he answered in a calm, reassuring tone. 'It's not far to the top now. Don't look down though.'

Gamely Jeanie struggled on. Above her, Colin sought out the easiest way and had to keep constantly remembering that the girl could not equal his reach or length of leg. Looking up, he saw the last feet would be difficult for any but the most experienced climber—and Jeanie was anything but that.

'C—Colin!' the girl croaked. 'I—I can't—go——'

'Just a few more feet, Jeanie lass,' the Scot answered. 'There's a ledge you can rest on until I reach the top and can help you up.'

How Jeanie made the ledge, she would never know. Somehow she managed to pull herself on to it. No more than eighteen inches wide, the ledge petered out within a few feet. By standing flattened against the wall, arms spreadeagled on the cold stone, Jeanie could rest her aching limbs. She felt the rope moving and managed to raise her eyes. Above her, Colin's kilt swung and his legs kicked for a moment. Then he disappeared from view and she felt a momentary panic.

'C—Colin!'

'I'm here, lass,' he answered, appearing at the edge. 'Very carefully get both hands on the rope. Slow and easy.'

Soothed and prompted by the calm voice, Jeanie followed the instructions. At first she thought that she would fall, but the rope gave her support. Looking down, Colin continued with his commands. Bracing her feet against the rock, Jeanie began to walk upwards as he pulled. Compared with the first part of the climb, the last twenty feet seemed child's play. Then she realised that it must have been sheer hell for the unaided Scot to go up.

Drawing in on the rope hand over hand, Colin found time to dart a glance at the entrance to the canyon. So far the men had not come into view. Up rose Jeanie and at last she gripped first one then both Colin's wrists. With a final tug, he swung her over the edge and on to welcome level ground.

'Colin!' Jeanie whispered and fell into his arms.

'You're safe now, lassie,' he replied. 'It's ove—— Get down!'

And saying the last words, Colin sank to the ground. He drew Jeanie down at his side, then peered cautiously over the edge. Backing off, he motioned the girl to follow him. They crept along the edge until they found a place from which they could see into the canyon without the danger of being seen. Looking towards the mouth of the canyon, Jeanie decided that they had not completed the climb any too soon. The riders came into sight and one of their number slipped off his horse to make a closer examination of the ground.

'I was right,' Jeanie breathed. 'Injuns and a Mex.'

'Jeanie!' Colin hissed at the squat-built Mexican. 'That's the man whose horse I shot in Fort Sawyer——'

'The one the Kid reckoned was Matteo Flores?' the girl gasped. 'Him and his brother must've tied in with the Tejas. Here they come into the canyon. We'll soon know if we've fooled them.'

'There's plenty of cover up here,' Colin commented, looking at the bush and rock-dotted land behind them. 'Let's see what they make of our disappearance first, then decide what to do next.'

Unknown to the Kid, three Tejas bucks had been ahead of the main body as scouts. When they had seen Jeanie's and Colin's departure from the camp, they took the news back to their companions. From their descriptions, the Flores brothers identified Colin. However the brothers ran into objections when they prepared to follow the Scot. On contacting the Tejas to form an alliance against Ma's party, Matteo's main point of persuasion had been that his gang carried Spencer rifles to counter the repeaters of the Texans. So, not unnaturally, the Tejas refused to let the brothers go off on a private hunt. The best the Indians would allow was for Matteo to take the three scouts, while Tiburcio and the other *bandidos* backed up the attack on the mustangers' camp.

Taking the trail out of sight of the camp, Matteo and his men followed it. They did not hurry, wanting to come upon Colin and Jeanie where the sound of shooting would not reach the camp. On approaching the canyon, they found their task made difficult by the coming and going of the mustangs.

'There's a horse!' the only Tejas with a firearm announced, pointing to Jeanie's dun.

'I can't see the man and girl,' Matteo growled, scanning the bottom of the canyon. 'Maybe they came out riding double.'

'None of the tracks show it if they did,' objected the taller of the lance-carrying braves. 'They're hiding in the canyon.'

Leaving their horses ground-hitched, the men advanced cautiously. While they studied every inch of the canyon's floor, none of them thought to look upwards. At the rocks where Jeanie had left her saddle, one of the lance-toting Tejas leapt forward excitedly and hauled it into view.

'They were here!' he yelled.

'We know that!' Matteo snorted. 'Only they're not in here now. Which way did they go?'

'We'd have seen them if they'd come out and crossed the open range,' Eats Anything, the man with the rifle announced. 'They must have climbed this slope.'

'Let's get after them!' whooped the second buck, dropping the saddle and moving towards the slope.

'Wooden Head is well named!' Eats Anything scoffed. 'If they are up there, they could kill us all as we climb.'

'I can't see any tracks,' Tommy Dog, the last Indian, commented. 'Maybe they went up the other side.'

'Look at that wall!' Matteo growled. 'They couldn't go up there. Either they went out of the entrance, or up this slope. Come on. We'll cut for sign out in front of the entrance. If we don't find any, we'll get on top and see if they're up there.'

Enough of the conversation had reached Jeanie's

ears for her to tell Colin something of the quartet's comments and plans. Then they watched Matteo lead the Tejas from the canyon and begin a careful scrutiny of the ground.

'I wish 'em luck, all bad,' Jeanie grinned as the men moved out of sight beyond the other side. 'We slickered 'em good, Colin boy.'

'My kinsman did much the same to the Hanoverians at the Pass of Ballater,' Colin replied. 'Only the Black Colonel took his horse with him.'

'Not up a wall like we climbed, even if he is your kin,' Jeanie objected.

'Maybe not,' the Scot smiled, then became sober again. 'I'm thinking it'd not be safe to start walking back just yet.'

'Let's find some place comfy to hide up in,' Jeanie suggested. 'The more we know about what they're figuring, the safer it'll be.'

Finding a hollow a short way from the edge, Colin and Jeanie took cover in it. For a time nothing happened, then they saw the four men riding towards the top at the other side of the canyon. Once more Matteo and the Tejas began their search for signs, covering the ground with a disconcerting, painstaking thoroughness.

'I'd say they're certain we didn't leave the canyon by the entrance,' Colin whispered.

'Yeah,' Jeanie hissed back. 'And when they don't find our sign up there, they're sure going to start thinking about this side. If they come round, they'll easy cut our trail and then we've got a fight on our hands.'

At first Jeanie and Colin thought that they would be in luck. Although the searchers were clearly puzzled by the lack of tracks, they seemed disinclined to accept the obvious answer. A heated debate took place, but enough of the words failed to reach Jeanie to prevent her knowing what was said. From what she could tell by the gestures and actions of the quartet, opinions were sharply divided on how the couple had escaped. Matteo appeared to favour making another examination of the land in front of the canyon, being at least partially supported by the two lance-carrying Tejas. However the man with the rifle objected and kept pointing to the other side. Finally he turned his horse and started to ride purposefully towards the blind end of the canyon. First the other Tejas, then Matteo followed. Catching up to the two men, the Mexican seemed to be continuing his arguments. While they talked, their companion drew steadily ahead of them.

'That does it,' Jeanie breathed. 'If we show ourselves, we'll be seen and they'll ride us down. Keep hid until they get into shooting range. Let 'em ride by if you can, then come up shooting.'

'I'll do that,' Colin agreed, knowing the situation did not call for fair play or sporting tactics. It would be kill or be killed, with Jeanie's life at stake as well as his own. 'Keep down and leave the fighting to me.'

'You'd best get those pipes unhitched,' Jeanie suggested as he drew and cocked the Dragoon. 'They might slip and tangle your arms.'

Deciding that the girl gave good advice, and aware of the need for complete freedom of movement, Colin began to slide the bagpipes' strap from over his shoulder. Although he moved with care, he allowed the pipes to show briefly above the rim of the hollow. For a moment the ribbons fluttered in the air and then were withdrawn without him realising his mistake. He learned about it soon enough.

Coming around the edge of the canyon in the lead of his companions, Eats Anything scanned the country about him with extra care. There had been doubts cast about the possibility of their victims being on the left side, despite the lack of tracks elsewhere. Eager to prove his reputation as a reader of sign, he wanted to locate the missing couple and prove that he had missed nothing down below. A slight movement jerked his attention to a hollow some fifty yards ahead. Something stirred in it, a flickering wave of colours unnatural to the surroundings. Whipping up his long-barrelled Mississippi rifle, Eats Anything took aim and fired.

Chapter Fifteen

When the bullet passed close above his head and kicked up dirt at the rear of the hollow, Colin knew their position had been discovered. Gripping the Dragoon in both hands, he wriggled up the side until he could rest his elbows on the level ground. That gave him a solid base from which to take aim and he proceeded to make the most of it.

Screeching out a triumphant war-yell, Eats Anything sent his horse bounding forward. He died before the animal had taken four strides. Carefully Colin sighted the Dragoon, knowing he had but five shots and wanting to make them all count. Pressing the trigger, he sent a bullet into the Indian's chest. Even as Eats Anything fell from the horse, Colin saw the other Indians coming to the attack.

Wooden Head dropped the point of his lance and sent his horse into a charging gallop. Despite carrying one, Tommy Dog did not share the Comanche and other horse-Indians' reverence for the lance. He regarded it as an inadequate kind of weapon when matched against a firearm. So he did not follow his companion's example. Instead he dropped his lance and reached over to snatch Matteo's Dragoon from its holster. Before the Mexican could prevent the theft, Dog headed in the direction of the hollow and started to shoot as if the revolver held sixty rather than six bullets in its cylinder.

Flame spurted from the Dragoon in Colin's hands and Wooden Head's horse began to fall. With an Indian's skill, the Tejas quit the dying animal's back and lit down on his feet. Still holding the lance, he watched Dog thunder by and began to run towards the hollow.

Firing his third shot, Colin saw Dog flinch but knew he had made a near miss. Nor did the fourth have better effect. Nearer tore Dog, the borrowed Dragoon spitting in his hand. Unfamiliar with the revolver and firing from the back of his horse, the man still came close to achieving his desires. Sliced by a bullet, the upper part of the feather in Colin's bonnet fell away. He heard the 'splat' as lead hummed by his left ear. Still he held his fire, intending to make a hit with the last load in the Dragoon.

Becoming aware of the danger, Dog fetched his horse to a sliding, turning halt. As the horse stopped, he tried to line the revolver down at the Scot. Only Colin was already laying his sights and shot first. Once more smoke swirled and the heavy old gun bucked to the recoil. A hole appeared between Dog's eyes and he pitched back over the far side of his horse. In falling, his lifeless hand tighted on the gun's butt and sent the last bullet it held ploughing into the ground.

Immediately after the shooting, Colin hurled himself out of the hollow with the intention of catching Dog's horse. However the animal went plunging away and Colin saw Wooden Head rushing in his direction. The sight of the lowered lance warned Colin that he held an empty gun and had need to defend himself. All the fighting spirit of his Highland blood raced wildly at the thought. Back over the centuries, the Farquharsons had been warriors second to none. The instincts of generations guided him in how he must act, backed by an even more primeval urge of the male to protect its mate. No longer was Colin the polite, well-bred young sportsman, but a wild Highlander of the kind which gave Britain some of its finest, bravest soldiers.

'Càrn na cuimhne!' Colin roared, bursting into full view of the charging Indian.

Around swung Colin's left arm, hurling the empty revolver at his attacker's face. Ducking to avoid the flying missile, Wooden Head staggered slightly. He was given no time to recover his balance. After leaving the Colt's butt, Colin's right hand flashed across to slip the dirk from its sheath. Following up in the path of the gun, he slapped the lance aside with his left hand.

'Càrn na cuimhne!'

Again the slogan of the Clan Farquharson rang through the Texas air. The eleven-inch long, tapering, double-edged blade rose in an upwards jab under the deflected war lance. Wooden Head croaked in agony as the needle-like spear point of the dirk spiked into his lower body. Instinct guided Colin's actions without the need for conscious thought. After half the blade had sunk into the Tejas' belly, the Scot tore it sideways to rip through the flesh until it came free.

Stepping aside, Colin let the stricken man blunder by him. The lance fell from Wooden Head's hands as he clutched at the hideous tear that laid open his stomach. Jeanie screamed as she saw the Indian lurch into view on the lip of the hollow. Then his legs buckled under him and he crashed downwards. Staring with horror-filled eyes, the girl jumped away from the gory body and began to back up the other slope.

Thundering hooves warned Colin that the danger was not yet over. In fact, he knew that he faced the most dangerous enemy of all. Not having seen the theft of Matteo's revolver, he expected to feel lead crash into him at any moment.

In addition to the loss of the revolver, Matteo no longer had a rifle. The Tejas had insisted that he left his Spencer with Cijar to add fire-power during the attack. Not that the *bandido* felt unduly concerned when he saw that the Scot held a revolver. Now that was empty and discarded. While the man in the skirt showed some skill in the use of a knife, Matteo carried an even more deadly edged weapon on his belt.

Snatching out the machete, Matteo guided his horse at Colin. Just as it seemed that Colin would be ridden down, he flung himself to the left before the horse and let it go by. Nor could Matteo bring the machete around in passing. Deftly the *bandido* reined his mount in a circle at the lip of the hollow and directed it into the attack again. Once more Colin stood his ground until the horse almost reached him before dodging in front of it and clear. Matteo's teeth drew back in a tight grin as he circled around for another attempt. No matter how he dressed, the man in the kilt was no fool or coward.

Reaching the top of the hollow, Jeanie watched the strange duel. Much as she wanted to help, she saw no way of doing so. To shout advice would distract Colin at a time when he needed all his wits about him. Nor could she think of anything to say. In fact, she considered that Colin was handling himself very well.

Matteo drove his horse forward for the third time. Instead of making it go at top speed, he kept its pace down. When the Scot darted clear, Matteo set his quickly devised plan into action. Throwing back his weight, he used the reins and a blow from the flat side of the machete's blade to twirl the horse around on its hind legs. Then he gave a yell, slammed his heels against the horse's ribs and caused it to leap in Colin's direction.

Taken by surprise, the Scot had no time to make a careful evasion. Instead he threw himself sideways hurriedly. Although the horse missed him, Colin felt his foot catch against a tuft of grass and he tripped. Throwing his left hand down as he fell, he broke his landing impact and did not sprawl at full length on the ground. However he found himself in a most dangerous position. There would be no chance of regaining his feet, for the *bandido* had already leapt to the ground. Throwing his left leg to the rear, Colin knelt on it.

Rushing up, Matteo launched a slash around designed to slice the Scot's head almost from his body. Still on his left knee, Colin brought up his right arm and interposed the dirk between himself and the down-lashing machete. Steel clashed on steel as the heavy blade of the machete met the dirk. Made of the finest steel available in Scotland, the long knife took and held the force of the impact. Slipping down, the machete's progress was halted by the haunches of the dirk's hilt. Instead of the quillon guard carried by most American fighting knives, the dirk had swollen haunches to protect its user's hand. How well they served showed when the sharp blade of the machete was prevented from descending.

Grimly Colin forced up at the machete and Matteo strained in an attempt to push the dirk down. Jeanie started to run around the hollow, meaning to throw herself on to the *bandido's* back and give Colin a chance to escape. Before she arrived, Colin achieved his own salvation. Using Matteo's downwards force as an aid to retaining his balance, Colin reached across to his right stocking top with his left hand. Gripping the hilt of the *sgian-dubh*, he drew it from its sheath. The short knife was no toy, or decorative miniature of the dirk, but a deadly weapon. Ending in a spear point, the blade carried an edge as sharp as a barber's razor and had been designed to be functional. Holding the *sgian-dubh* with the blade below the heel of the hand, Colin chopped upwards. His aim was true and the knife bit home between the *bandido's* spread-apart legs.

Pain tore through Matteo, bringing a screech from his lips. In attempt to escape from the agony, he jerked an involuntary pace to the rear. Like a flash Colin thrust himself erect. Gliding forward, he fetched the dirk around in a savage cross slash. Raking across Matteo's throat, the sharp edge laid it open almost to the bone. Discarding his machete, the *bandido* spun around and crashed across Dog's body.

Slowly the wild, savage elation of the mortal combat ebbed away from Colin. The red mists of battle cleared from his head and he looked half amazed at the destruction he had wrought.

Dashing up, babbling queries about his well-being, Jeanie flung herself into his arms. Just in time he let the two knives fall from his hands, then crushed her to him. Lifting her face towards his, the full flood of Jeanie's emotions burst and she began to sob almost hysterically. Colin scooped her into his arms, cradling her against his chest until the spasm passed. Then he set her on her feet and held her at arms' length.

'It's all over, lassie,' he whispered. 'But I'm thinking we'd best get away from here in case there are more of them about.'

Sucking down a sob, Jeanie fought to regain her normal attitude of self-possession.

'Sure we had,' she agreed and worry flickered across her face. 'Don't tell Ma or anybody how I acted just now, will you?'

'You don't need to ask me that, lass,' Colin told her. 'It's over and forgotten. Where are their horses?'

On turning to look, Jeanie and Colin found that the horses had continued running after losing their riders. Already even Matteo's mount was too far away for them to hope to catch it.

'We've got a long walk ahead,' Jeanie sighed. 'And I surely hate walking.'

'If you get tired, I'll carry you,' Colin promised. 'What about your saddle?'

'It'll do there until we can get a hoss to tote it back. Get your knives and gun while I fetch the rest of our gear.'

Picking up his Dragoon, Colin looked at Matteo. However he could not bring himself to search the body in the hope of finding ammunition. So he gathered and cleaned his knives while Jeanie collected the rope and bagpipes from the hollow.

'I could get that Indian's rifle if he's got powder and shot on him,' Colin suggested when the girl joined him.

'You could,' she admitted. 'But I wouldn't want to chance using any Injun's gun. They're likely to blow up in your face most any time.'

'It won't be so bad when some of our folk come looking for us,' Colin remarked, walking with Jeanie in search of a place to climb down to the land below.

'Something tells me that they can't come looking,' Jeanie answered soberly. 'If the Tejas're siding the Flores boys, its likely to be for an attack on our camp.'

'It's me the brothers are after,' Colin pointed out.

'Yeah. And only Matteo come after you. The Tejas'd want something afore they'd help out. After the way you boys handled them, I'd say their price'd be that Tiburcio and the rest of the gang helped them against us.'

'You think they're attacking the camp then?'

'It's likely. But the Kid was dogging them and'd get back word of what's happening to Dusty. Pappy picked that camp because it's a good place to hole up and fight. We held off and plumb discouraged a big bunch of Kiowa bad-hats there one time and with only one Henry.'

'Then your mother and the others have a chance,' Colin sighed.

'I'd say better'n a fair one with Dusty Fog along. That boy's one whole he-coon in a fight and his pards're no slouches. Still, sooner we're back there the better for all of us.'

Once down on the level ground, Colin allowed Jeanie to lead the way. She made for the *bosque* and they crossed the stream at the point where the horses had carried them over on the way out. Through the trees, Jeanie continued to keep almost to the line taken by them during the wild chase from the camp. Although they kept alert, they neither saw nor heard anything to disturb them. Then the distant crackle of gun-fire brought them to a halt.

'It's from the camp!' Jeanie said and started forward. 'Come on——!'

'Slow down, lass!' Colin ordered, catching her arm and bringing her to a halt. 'We can't run all the way and arrive in any condition to fight.'

'That's for sure,' Jeanie admitted. 'Only Ma and the others——'

'I'm worrying about them too, lass. But it'll do them no good if we rush up and are taken prisoner by those red heathens.'

'How do we play it then?'

'Keep walking at a steady pace, watching our step all the way. Once we get close enough to see what's happening, we can decide what to do for the best.'

Listening, Jeanie told herself that Colin had a damned good grasp of the situation and had put up the only sensible idea. With that decided, she allowed him to set the speed at which they walked and held down her impatience. Every one of her previous misgivings about the Scot had completely disappeared. There was a man any Texas gal would be right pleased to marry, happen he got around to asking her. Even if he did not, Jeanie decided that the end result would be the same.

'It's a free country,' she mused. 'So why can't a gal do the asking if the feller won't?'

Walking on, she put aside her flippant thought. The shooting died away, then welled up for a short time and faded off. Although the odd shots cracked out, the volume of fire did not rise again. Having been through Indian attacks before, Jeanie guessed that the assault had failed. Most likely the Indians were backed off, leaving a few men to harass the defenders while the rest re-made their medicine. The idea gained strength as they drew nearer and she could hear the reports better. Sharp cracks from Henry rifles intermingled with the deeper growl of large caliber weapons.

At last the nearer shots sounded from over the rim up which they were climbing. So they stalked cautiously upwards until they could peer over the top. Lying flat, they could see the camp and were heartened by what they saw. At least eight Indians and two Mexicans were scattered before the defenders' position and the watchers could see no signs of casualties among their friends. A further pair of Mexicans and a handful of Tejas crouched behind various pieces of cover, bombarding the camp. Even as Jeanie and Colin watched, the Kid rose slightly from where he lay under the chuckwagon. His Winchester spat and one of the Mexicans lurched out of hiding then collapsed.

The remainder of the Indians gathered around Tiburcio Flores and another Mexican Colin and Jeanie recognised.

'Cijar!' the girl spat out. 'How did that no-good *pelados* get tied in with Flores and the Injuns?'

'I couldn't say,' Colin answered dryly. 'Right now, I'm more interested in finding out what they're talking about.'

'Yah!' Jeanie sniffed, poking her tongue out at him. 'So sneak up on 'em and listen.'

'That's what I was thinking of doing, lass,' Colin informed her.

'Colin!' Jeanie gasped, realising he was serious. 'It'll be risky as hell.'

'I've stalked deer in the Highlands, lassie. Those feller're no sharper in the eyes and ears than a good stag.'

'Let's go then. And don't tell me "no". We haven't time to argue it out—and you can't speak Spanish.'

That was a decisive point, even if Colin had wished to leave Jeanie behind. It would be of no use him moving unobserved to a place where he could hear the men and then be unable to understand them. So he looked around, picking out the safest position for them to use. Along the rim there was a large clump of dogwood bushes which would fill their needs. Nodding to it, Colin received a smile of confirmation from the girl. Carefully backing from the rim, they made their way to the bushes and eased their way under the shelter of the foliage until able once more to see the Mexicans and Indians. Not more than seventy yards separated them and they could hear all the others said.

'Flores wants them to attack again,' Jeanie whispered. 'Only the chief allows they've lost enough men already and's set to pull out.'

'It may be all right then,' Colin breathed back.

'No. Flores's got Cijar telling the Injuns about all the good things they'll get from the wagons. Guns, powder, bullets, the hosses, food. Dirty, stinking son-of-a-bitch. He's got them interested again.'

'The black-hearted devil!'

'Which one of 'em? Anyways, the chief still reckons they're not chancing another attack. Now Flores allows to have a right smart notion. He wants them to make a rush just after sun-down.'

'That'd be a good time for it,' Colin admitted. 'But Dusty's sure to be expecting them to do just that.'

'Maybe not,' Jeanie answered. 'Injuns don't do much fighting in the dark. They figure the Great Spirit might not find 'em if they get killed at night.'

Silently they listened to the argument carried on between Flores and the chief. Even Colin could see that the Mexican was making his point and Jeanie confirmed it.

'He's got it all figured out. They pull back over the rim and make like they're fixing to settle down for the night. Just do enough to let our folks know they're still on hand. Then him and his men'll take the Spencers and move around to the side. Soon as the sun drops, they'll start shooting and the Injuns'll go down the slope like the devil-after-a-yearling.'

More talk followed, which Jeanie said was a discussion on whether the attack would be good medicine or not. At last it was decided to put the plan into operation. Leaving the few men armed with rifles to hold the defender's attention, the remainder rode over the rim. They passed within a few yards of the bushes, never suspecting Jeanie and Colin lay hidden so near.

'What'll we do?' Jeanie asked, her mouth close to Colin's ear in the interests of added silence. 'Charging down like that, they'll at least run off all our hosses.'

'We can't do anything yet,' Colin replied. 'How will they make the attack?'

'On their hosses, if I know Injuns.'

'If they do, we'll see what their horses make of pipe music,' Colin stated.

Settling down as comfortably as they could manage, Colin and Jeanie prepared to wait out the long hours until dark. Colin placed his dirk close to his hand and gave Jeanie the *sgian-dubh*, so that they would have the means to defend themselves if discovered.

None of the enemy came near the bushes. However a few braves rode off in different directions. Jeanie guessed that they had been sent out to gather food for the rest of the band. One of the hunters brought back something unexpected when he galloped up leading four horses.

Flores recognised his brother's mount and started to demand that a search be made. Having become enthusiastic over the idea of an unexpected night attack, the Tejas chief refused to let the Mexican go. Instead he sent off six of his own men. They returned shortly before sun-down and told Tiburcio of Matteo's death. Learning that the braves had not tried to track down the man who did the killing, Flores cursed them. Their insistence that they thought *he* would wish to avenge the death of his brother struck Tiburcio as a mite unconvincing, but he accepted it. Realising that there would be insufficient light for him to search for the girl and the man in the skirt, he gave his attention to preparing for the attack.

Slowly the sun sank beyond the western horizon. In its last light, the Mexicans took their rifles and horses to the position from which they would send covering fire into the camp. Gathering their mounts, the Indians formed up behind the rim and waited for their chief's order to attack.

In the bushes, Colin knelt and took up his pipes. Jeanie kissed him lightly on the cheek as he tucked the bag under his arm and rested the raised pipes on his shoulder. Giving the girl a comforting smile, Colin filled his lungs with air. Then he placed the chanter in his mouth and began to blow.

Chapter Sixteen

The noise caused by the horses moving restlessly and riders muttering drowned the first murmur of the pipes. Slowly the sound grew louder, rising through the night with all its wild beauty of tone. Never had Colin played as he did crouching among the dogwood bushes at the side of the woman he loved and whose mother and friends he sought to save.

If the mustangers' horses had displayed aversion towards the tones of the bagpipes, it was nothing to how the Indian ponies reacted—and the Tejas showed that they too had little taste for Highland music. Snorts of terror broke out as the skirling wails reached the ponies, mingling with the startled yells of the Indians. Never had the Tejas heard such a sound and they formed their own interpretations of what caused it. Despite Flores' assurances, none of the braves had felt happy or comfortable about breaking the age-old tradition by fighting in the dark. So, hearing the—to them—unearthly noise lifting from so close at hand, they decided it must be an expression of the Great Spirit's wrath at their impiety.

With the music ringing louder, the horses started to pitch and tried to run away. Three braves were thrown from their mounts in the ensuing chaos. Then the whole band began to scatter. Scooping up their un-horsed companions, the Tejas lit out as fast as they could go.

'Damned heathens!' Colin snorted, lowering the

chanter for a moment. 'Don't they know good music when they hear it?'

'It sure looks that way,' Jeanie replied, hugging him. 'But I like it. What do we do now?'

'Go down to see how your mother and the others are,' Colin answered. 'Come on, lassie. I'll pipe you home.'

Picking up Colin's dirk, Jeanie followed him from the bushes. If she had known more about Highland music, the girl would have been highly delighted as she marched down the slope at the Scot's side. The tune Colin played was the one his clan used, when a chief brought home his bride.

In the camp, Dusty and the others heard the pipes beyond the rim, then listened to the sounds which followed the music.

'Whee dogie!' the Kid said. 'That danged fool Colin's scaring their hosses.'

'Come on!' Dusty snapped. 'We'd best get up there and help him. Stay put, Ma, we'll get up to them.'

Leaving the places from which they had made their effective fight, Dusty, Mark and the Kid ran towards the slope. At any moment they expected to hear shooting or other sounds to tell them that Colin and Jeanie were fighting for their lives against the Tejas enraged by losing the horses.

Crouching among the clump of bushes, Flores and his last two men also heard the pipes and departure of the Indians. Cijar and Gomez let out startled exclamations, crossing themselves in superstitious awe and seemed on the verge of bolting. While Flores had no more idea than his companions of what caused the wailing, his nerve held. Snarling at the others to keep still, he prepared to enforce the order with lead if necessary.

'Wha—What was it?' Cijar croaked as the pipes droned into silence.

'The wind, or something,' Flores replied. 'Nothing more.'

For all his light dismissal of the sound, Flores knew just what it meant. His Indian allies had fled and, after such a scare, would be unlikely to return. When the wailing began again, he turned his eyes in its direction. However a movement from Gomez distracted him.

'Look!' the *bandido* hissed, sighting his rifle towards the camp. 'Some of them are coming out.'

Peering through the darkness, Flores saw the three fast-moving figures. He recognised them as the deadly trio of Texans who had been such a decisive factor in the defence of the camp. In which case he had no wish to draw their attention his way. More so when one of them was *Cabrito*, famed for his ability at fighting in the darkness.

'Don't shoot!' Flores spat out. 'Do you want them to know we're here?'

When he had it pointed out to him, Gomez also saw the danger. Shooting in the dark would be chancy and, if he missed, would alert *Cabrito* to their presence. So he lowered the rifle and looked at his leader.

'What are we going to do, *patrôn*?'

'What we came here to do. Kill the man with the skirt. As soon as it's light, we'll start looking for him.'

'There's somebody else on the slope!' Cijar whispered. 'I think it's the man and the Schell girl!'

After staring for a moment, Flores nodded in agreement, 'It is! The son-of-a-whore must have made the noise and frightened the Tejas.'

'Are we going to attack them, *patrôn*?' Gomez inquired in a voice which showed no pleasure at the idea.

'Not now,' Flores decided. Seething with rage though he might be, the *bandido* leader could still think. Much the same objections were against an attack as there had been to shooting at the Texans. So he was willing to wait for a better opportunity, and if possible, create it himself. 'Come on, let's get the horses and ride.'

'You don't mean to avenge your brothers?' asked Cijar.

'Of course I do!' Flores snarled. 'And I've an idea how to do it. If I can't get to him, I'll have to make him come to me.'

Colin received a hero's welcome on his arrival at the camp and the acclaim grew greater when Jeanie told how he had saved her. Having left the others to make a search of the surrounding area, the Kid arrived back in time to hear the girl say that Colin had killed another member of the Flores family. Then the dark youngster reported on his findings.

'They've all pulled out,' he announced.

'Then we've seen the last of Flores?' Colin asked. 'Or was he killed?'

'He warn't,' the Kid replied. 'And we ain't seed the last of him. Tiburcio and his two yahoos didn't go with the Injuns. They lit out for the south. With you downing Matteo, Tiburcio'll be even more set on taking your hair. I'd say Matteo was the only one he gave shucks for.'

'We'd best make ready for him then,' Dusty stated. 'Set out pickets, Lon. Make sure they don't sneak back again. Then we'll have a fire built and a meal made while we tend to the horses.'

Leaving the Kid to handle the placing of guards, Dusty set all the others to work. Two *mesteneros* had been killed and three wounded, none seriously. Ma attended to the wounds and left the rest of the cleaning up in Dusty's capable hands. By the time April and Fernán had the fire going and food cooked, the horses had been separated, *sarprimas* replaced on the mustangs, saddle-mounts taken to the picket line and herdmares driven off to range feed.

The night passed without incident and the following day was to be spent in clearing up after the attack. However the Kid returned from a scouting mission with strange news.

'One of Flores' boys's coming,' he said, halting his white stallion at Dusty's side. 'Got him a white rag on the end of his gun barrel.'

'Best see what he wants,' Dusty decided. 'Get everybody in cover ready for trouble, Ma.'

'Yo!' the woman answered and gave the orders.

'Any sign of the rest of them, Lon?' Dusty inquired, watching the preparations for defence.

'Nary a flicker,' the Kid answered. 'Them Tejas won't've stopped running yet and Flores' man's alone.'

When Gomez rode into sight, he found the camp prepared to hold off any attack. Halting his horse, he stared at the levelled rifles and waved his white flag to make sure that it could be seen.

'Come ahead slow and easy!' Dusty ordered in Spanish. 'If there's any trickery, you're dead.'

'No tricks, *señor*!' Gomez promised hurriedly. 'My *patrôn* has sent a message to the man in the skirt who killed his brothers.'

Riding forward, still displaying his piece of white rag prominently, Gomez came to a halt before Ma's wagon. Followed by Jeanie, Colin emerged from beneath it but Dusty ordered the others to remain in their places. Taking the rifle from the *bandido*, Dusty went to the Scot's side and asked what Gomez had in mind. Much to Dusty surprise, the man began to speak in passable English.

'My *patrôn*, Señor Tiburcio Flores, sent me to say that he has no quarrel with anybody here except the man who killed his brothers.'

'That's right neighbourly of him,' Dusty drawled. 'If it's all he wanted to tell us, you've had a ride for nothing.'

'Señor Flores says if the man who wears a skirt will meet and fight him at the deserted village to the south, he will make no more trouble for you.'

'And if he won't?' asked Dusty before Colin could speak.

'Much as he would dislike doing it, *señor*, my *patrôn* would have to make plenty trouble for all of you.'

'What kind of trouble?'

'You hunt wild horses. He would burn your

corrals, scatter the *mestenas*, have your *mesteneros* killed from ambush——'

'And we'd just sit back and let him?' Dusty said sardonically.

'While you hunt us, you can't hunt your horses, *señor*,' Gomez pointed out. 'And Señor Flores is a patient man. If he has to, he will go back to Mexico to gather more men. Then one day he will return for his brother's killer.'

'That figures,' the Kid put in.

'Señor Flores said for me to tell the one who wears a skirt that a true man does not hide behind his friends.' Gomez continued, looking directly at Colin.

'I hide behind no man!' Colin blazed, stepping forward. 'Tell yon murdering heathen you serve that I'll fight him anywhere and at any time.'

'Colin!' Jeanie gasped, moving to his side.

'There's no other way, lassie,' Colin told her gently. 'If I don't fight him, we'll never be free from that murderous blackguard.'

'He's right, Jeanie,' the Kid said without taking his attention from the country about him. 'Even if it doesn't come now, Flores'll not forget. Colin can't live safe in Texas while Tiburcio's alive.'

The girl gave no sign of hearing the words. Instead she clung to Colin's arm and looked into his face. 'I—I don't want to lose you.'

'Do you still think I need wet-nursing, lass?' the Scot asked.

'N—No. It's not that. You can't trust Flores to play straight.'

'Now you don't reckon that *we'd* let Colin ride down there on his lonesome, do you?' Dusty put in and turned to Gomez. 'We'll be riding with our *amigo* to the village——'

'Damn it, Dusty!' Colin barked. 'The man's challenged me——'

'Sure,' agreed the small Texan. 'Only we're going along to see there's no tricks. Hey, *hombre*, tell your *patrôn* the three of us will stop outside the village as long as his men do the same. If they cut in, so do we.'

'It's that way, or I'll shoot you in the leg afore I'll let you go, Colin,' Jeanie stated. 'I mean it!'

'I believe you do,' the Scot smiled and gave his attention to Gomez. 'Tell Flores that I had no choice but kill his brothers and I'm sorry I had to do it. If he won't have it any other way, I'll face him man to man.'

'I will tell him, *señor*,' Gomez promised. 'But it will not change his mind.'

'We'll be there at sun-down tomorrow,' Dusty said. 'Tell Flores that we'll want to see you and his other man out the back of the village before Colin comes in alone.'

'*Sí, señor*. Can I go now?'

'We've nothing more to say,' Dusty answered. '*Vamos, pronto!*'

'You want for me to trail along after him?' the Kid inquired as Gomez mounted up and rode away.

'I don't reckon so,' Dusty replied. 'There's work to be done around here and anyways, we'll be ready if they try to lay for us on the way there tomorrow. And if Flores' fixing any smart play, we'll ride into the village with Colin.'

Nobody spoke much for a time after Dusty's decision not to let the Kid follow Gomez. While the *mesteneros* went about their various tasks, the Texans gathered at the fire with Ma, Jeanie and Colin. They all knew that a fight with Flores could not be avoided and wondered how the young Scot would fare against an experienced man like the *bandido*. April walked over, bringing a tray loaded with mugs of coffee.

'I've allus found it's easier to think over a pot of Arbuckle's,'* the blonde remarked. 'And there's some thinking needs doing right now.'

'How will he fight do you think, Dusty?' Colin asked after a slight pause.

'Could be any way,' the small Texan answered. 'He had a Spencer rifle yesterday, so he might use that.'

**Arbuckle's:* the most popular brand of coffee in the early West.

'You'd best take your Henry along,' the Kid suggested.

'I'm a better shot with the old double,' Colin replied.

'Then take that,' Dusty said. 'You'll have your Dragoon, but stay out of a close-up, draw-and-shoot if you can.'

At the mention of the Dragoon, Jeanie stiffened slightly and looked hard towards the gun in Colin's holster. Then she turned and whispered into her mother's ear. Surprise flickered briefly across Ma's face, to be replaced by a faint smile as she nodded in agreement to her daughter's request. Standing up, Jeanie walked away from the fire. Colin watched her go in a puzzled manner, unable to understand why she went without an explanation.

'I'd say he'll fight shy of using a knife after you finished Matteo with one,' Mark said as Jeanie swung out of sight into the living room. 'But you'd best have that Arkansas toothpick along just in case.'

'Aye,' Colin answered in a distracted manner.

Jeanie appeared at the end of the wagon and dropped to the ground. 'Colin,' she called.

Straightening himself from squatting on his heels, Colin strode towards the girl. He saw that she had her hands behind her back but gave it no thought. There was a light in her eyes which held his full attention.

'What is it?' he asked.

'I love you,' she replied. 'No. Let me finish. I treated you mean and said some bad things when we first met——'

'I deserved them——'

'Please, Colin!' she breathed. 'I'm sorry for everything I said and—and—— Here, when you go after Flores, tomorrow, take this.'

Bringing her right hand into sight, she held her father's ivory-handled Dragoon Colt in Colin's direction.

Chapter Seventeen

'Damned if I'd've thought it, but it looks like Flores's playing it straight,' the Ysabel Kid commented as he rode with Dusty, Mark and Colin towards the deserted village. 'Look over the other side there.'

On a ridge almost half a mile beyond the village, two sombrero and serape-clad figures sat their horses under the branches of a big old cottonwood tree. They were sufficiently far from the buildings to be out of the game ahead and there was not enough cover for them to dismount and sneak back to help their boss.

'He could have more men on hand,' Mark pointed out.

'Could,' admitted the Kid. 'But I'm betting he hasn't. He's lost some since the hold-up and likely had others quit on him. And he'd've brought every man he had when he jumped the camp. Nope, I'd say those two're all the help he's got left.'

'I go along with you, Lon,' Dusty said. 'Flores wouldn't play it this way if he had more men.'

'Then it's just him and me,' Colin put in quietly.

'That's how it looks,' Dusty agreed. 'On——'

'I just saw a smidgin of a flicker down there!' interrupted the Kid. 'Either Flores's sending mirror signals, or he's watching us through field-glasses.'

'Mostly likely watching us,' Mark guessed. 'There's nobody around for him to signal to.'

'We can't go much farther, Colin,' Dusty warned. 'But if there's any hint of more of them around, hunt for a hole and we'll come running.'

'A stupid, dead hero's no use to Jeanie,' Mark went on. 'Sides which, think about us three.'

'How do you mean?' Colin asked, sounding puzzled.

'Happen you got shot that ways, it'd be *us* who'd have to go back and face her,' the blond giant explained, holding out a big right hand. 'Good luck, *amigo*.'

After shaking hands with the Texans, Colin went forward alone. He sat his saddle with tense alertness, the heavy caliber double-rifle's butt resting on his knee and barrels pointing into the air. Riding in his holster was the ivory-handled Dragoon Colt, while the dirk hung at his other side.

Approaching the edge of the village, Colin dismounted. Going into a fight, he preferred to be on foot rather than riding. So he left the horse standing with its reins trailing and walked forward. He held the rifle ready for use and looked along the street. Under the circumstances, the crumbling buildings seemed extra stark and almost menacing. However Colin saw nothing of his waiting enemy. Then he became aware that a man had come from a house at the other end of the street. With a feeling of shock, Colin realised that it was Gomez. The man wore neither sombrero not serape but carried a Spencer rifle.

Amusement flickered on Gomez's face as he brought the Spencer to his shoulder and commenced to take a leisurely aim. Everything appeared to be going just as Flores had planned. Clearly the dummies, dressed in spare clothing and mounted on horses picked up during the return from the fatal attack on the camp, had fooled the Texans—even *Cabrito*. More than that, the *bandido* leader had correctly predicted how the man in the skirt would be armed. Thinking back to how Vicente had been killed, Tiburcio decided that Colin Farquharson would use a shotgun. So he had made his arrangements accordingly, placing Gomez at the far end of the street with orders to make use of the Spencer's superior range.

The *bandido* felt no great concern as he saw his victim also raising a weapon. At something over a hundred yards, the nine balls from the shotgun would have spread so that only luck might guide one his way. With that thought in mind, Gomez saw no need to hurry in taking aim and made the last mistake of his mis-spent life.

Swiftly, yet carefully, Colin lined the double barrels of the gun on Gomez and squeezed its forward trigger. A heavy powder charge burned and the rifle boomed like a small cannon in the stillness of the evening. Speeding through the air, a .600 caliber bullet glanced from the barrel of the Spencer and struck the centre of the *bandido's* forehead. Lifted from his feet by the impact, his skull a shattered ruin, Gomez crashed backwards.

Even as he fired, Colin caught a movement from the corner of his eye. Like a flash he swivelled around and dropped to his left knee in turning. Lead slapped the air by his head and he saw Cijar framed in the window of the nearest building. Finding himself detected and having missed with his shot, the *mestenero* jerked back behind the wall. He was content to be out of Colin's sight and waited for Tiburcio to intervene before attempting to show himself.

Again the heavy rifle bellowed. The large caliber bullet drove through the adobe wall as if it had been so much paper and struck Cijar. Churning into his arm, the lead passed through to his chest. Giving a choking cry, the man staggered in a circle, tripped and fell.

A shot crashed from along the street and Colin felt a seering pain on his left arm. Letting the empty rifle fall, he threw himself sideways and twisted to face his next assailant. Face distorted with rage, Tiburcio

Flores hurled himself into the centre of the street. Colin could see the smoke-wrapped shape approaching and bullets flew around him. Landing on the street, he brought the Dragoon from its holster. Even as Flores came to a halt so as to shoot straighter, Colin fired. Hit in the centre of the chest, the *bandido* fell, screaming curses.

At the first hint of treachery, Dusty, Mark and the Kid had set their horses moving. However they had almost half a mile to cover and by the time they arrived, the last of the Flores gang lay dying. Getting back to his feet, Colin shook his left hand and worked its throbbing fingers. Blood dribbled from where Flores' bullet had raked a furrow along his forearm.

'He had men with him,' Colin told the Texans when they arrived.

'And they didn't do him one lil bit of good,' replied the Kid. 'You sure you don't have Comanche blood, Colin? You sure fight like a *Nemenuh*.'

'Move aside, you danged *Tshaoh*!' Mark snorted. 'Leave me fix up this forty-four caliber man's arm.'

'Yes sir, *amigo*,' Dusty went on. 'You've earned being called a forty-four caliber man, Colin.'

Not even the fact that he had gained what amounted to an accolade from the Texans equalled the pleasure Colin felt over how Jeanie greeted him on his return. Rushing forward regardless of the watching *mesteneros*, she threw her arms about his neck and had to be reassured that he was not seriously hurt. With that attended to Colin went to Ma and took the Dragoon from his holster.

'Keep it, son,' she said, glancing at Jeanie and smiling. 'Nobody'll say you're not man enough to carry it now.'

That night Jeanie and Colin strolled together along the stream's banks. After discussing the hunt which would start the following morning, they both tried to bring up the subject each wanted to air. Jeanie had never been long on patience and Colin smiled as he waited to see how she would handle the situation. At last she reached down to stroke the rough material of his kilt.

'Colin,' she whispered. 'What *do* you wear under this?'

'That's something a Scot can only tell his wife,' he replied, taking her hand in his.

'All right,' she smiled, nestling closer to him. 'If that's the only way I can find out, I'll marry you.'

'I thought you'd never ask me,' Colin grinned. 'Let's go and tell Ma.'

Walking towards the camp at the side of her forty-four caliber man, Jeanie gave a little chuckle. Let him think that he had tricked her into doing the proposing if it made him happy. She had known the answer to her question ever since following Colin up the canyon wall.